SAT

All around him, people were screaming as the ground moved under him, a terrifying feeling. The one thing people always counted on, always knew would be there, was the ground beneath their feet and the sky over their head. When the ground begins to toss about, like a giant shrugging his shoulders, it so distorts one's worldview that one half expects the sky to crash down.

And now the screams of the people were mingling with a roar like the gates of hell being hurled open upon massive hinges. The pier shook violently, and Chuck was hurled off his feet. Falling was nothing new for him—he'd spent hours during aikido training doing nothing but falling. Even now, with the earth buckling under him, his old instincts took hold and he executed a perfect roll, coming back up to his feet. He looked around frantically for the priest, shouting his name.

He spotted the priest, over by the water, hanging on desperately to the iron railings. The priest was screaming something, over and over, and Chuck couldn't hear what the frantic clergyman was saying. Then he lip-read enough to make it out—

"It's him!" the priest was shouting. "It's him . . ."

PSI-MAN

THE CHAOS KID

Peter David

ACE BOOKS, NEW YORK

This is a work of fiction. Names, characters, places, and incidents are
either the product of the author's imagination or are used fictitiously,
and any resemblance to actual persons, living or dead, business
establishments, events, or locales is entirely coincidental.

PSI-MAN: THE CHAOS KID

An Ace Book / published by arrangement with
the author

PRINTING HISTORY
Diamond edition / July 1991
Ace mass-market edition / July 2000

All rights reserved.
Copyright © 1991 by Charter Communications, Inc.

This book may not be reproduced in whole or in part,
by mimeograph or any other means, without permission.
For information address: The Berkley Publishing Group,
a division of Penguin Putnam Inc.,
375 Hudson Street, New York, New York 10014.

The Penguin Putnam Inc. World Wide Web site address is
http://www.penguinputnam.com

Check out the ACE Science Fiction & Fantasy newsletter
and much more on the Internet at Club PPI!

ISBN: 0-441-00745-7

ACE®
Ace Books are published
by The Berkley Publishing Group,
a division of Penguin Putnam Inc.,
375 Hudson Street, New York, New York 10014.
ACE and the "A" design are trademarks
belonging to Penguin Putnam Inc.

PRINTED IN THE UNITED STATES OF AMERICA

10 9 8 7 6 5 4 3 2 1

Christmas Week 2021

1

A light rain had been falling steadily on San Francisco for some hours as the low-slung car rolled slowly up to the empty telephone booth.

Alex Romanova swung open the door and stepped out carefully, being fastidiously certain not to step ankle-deep into the water that had collected at curbside. Glancing right and left to make certain that no one was following—for this was the fourth phone booth visited this evening, a practice generated by the type of paranoia that kept good agents like Romanova alive—Alex went to the phone and picked up the receiver.

A quick slide of a white Card through the vertical magnetic track on the phone got Alex a ready dial tone. Alex's fingers quickly tapped out a phone number at which no one lived. The phone number connected to a tie line, which in turn connected into a computer secreted somewhere in Fargo, North Dakota, which in turn sent the call somewhere else through a secured line.

From there it was channeled still farther and, for all the

agent knew, bounced off the moon before finally ending up ringing a phone on some faraway desk somewhere, the exact location of which not even Alex knew. This was a safety measure for all concerned.

Genady Korsakov picked it up.

"Alex?" said Korsakov.

Alex blinked in mild surprise. Genady Korsakov's abilities were well documented in files that were intended for certain eyes only. Even so, dealing with Korsakov one-on-one could be most disconcerting.

"Yes, it's me."

"What do you have to report? Is he the wild talent that we believe him to be?"

Alex nodded, forgetting momentarily that Korsakov couldn't see through the phone. Hell, maybe he could at that. "I believe so."

"Belief isn't good enough."

"Yes, well, dying isn't good enough, either," said Alex, sounding a bit cross. The rain was starting to come down harder, soaking Alex's hair. Romanova pulled the raincoat more tightly closed, but it didn't seem to help appreciably. "From everything that I've observed, Olivetti is everything that preliminary intelligence is cracking him up to be."

"Recommendations?"

"Kill him."

Korsakov was silent for a long moment upon hearing that. Alex knew that it wasn't what he had expected to hear. "Repeat, Romanova," he said slowly.

"Kill him," came the crisp reply again.

"Do you have any idea what you're saying, Alex?" To Alex's surprise, his voice actually seemed to be pleading slightly. "The amount of power he represents . . ."

"Would put us over and above the Americans, yes, I know," said Alex. "And it doesn't matter a damn if young Matthew Olivetti winds up destroying everything."

Another long pause. "As powerful as that."

"Yes."

"I want him."

Alex Romanova sighed. "I would advise against it."

"I know what your advice is. Now I'm telling you what your orders are. Teenagers are malleable. Do what you can to manipulate him."

"Frankly, I'm uncomfortable just being in the same state with him."

The longest pause of all. "I'm stunned, Romanova," came the curt response. "Stunned that you, an accomplished Russian agent, would be so intimidated by one boy."

Romanova muttered a low Russian curse.

"What was that?" demanded Genady.

Romanova knew that Genady had heard perfectly. "Nothing. I'm not intimidated. But I'm just trying to be cautious and smart."

"Then you can live out your years as a bookkeeper or pastry chef," said Genady. "But someone in your line of work has to be willing to take chances, even if they involve unpleasant situations."

"How about suicidal situations?"

"Those as well."

"Thank you for clarifying that for me, Genady, especially since you are safe an ocean away," said Alex, feeling nervy since there was little doubt in the agent's mind that this mission would be the last one of this lifetime.

Genady paused again. Alex had noticed that long ago about Korsakov. He never hurried in his statements, but thought matters over and spoke deliberately and carefully. Never a wasted breath or a hurried word.

"Alex, remember this old saying," and Genady did not sound entirely unsympathetic. " 'There are bold men, and there are old men, but there are no old, bold men.' "

There was a soft click, and the line went dead.

Romanova chuckled softly and said, to no one in particular, "Why am I not especially comforted by that?"

2

The next day was a school day and virtually every kid on the field had homework that they hadn't completed. But they tried not to let the arbitrary shackles that adults habitually hung around them get in the way of their good time. Sides had been chosen up and the two teams quickly split to go to the opposite ends of the makeshift football field. There were no nice, neat, and tidy lines marking off ten-yard grids, or high, sparkling goalposts.

Instead, trees served as markers, guaranteeing wildly disparate and uneven boundaries, as well as inevitable arguments over who had done what to whom and where. Those arguments, of course, were most of the fun of the game.

The only one not having fun was Paulie.

Paulie, the smallest, the runt of the litter—the smallest of the ten- to twelve-year-olds dispersing on the field— wailed forlornly, "What about me?"

The other kids stopped, contemplating him a moment and giving a collective sigh of frustration. The teams were even at nine each, and besides, no one wanted the kid. He was constantly shoving his glasses into place, and his haircut was poor, and he smelled funny, and what the hell was he doing there anyway? Sometimes they just yelled at him to go home, but he never did. At best he would go off into a corner of the field and sulk, annoying everybody.

Finally the oldest and tallest of the kids, Bobby, shook his head and said, "We'll take him. That'll give us ten. That okay with you guys?"

The decision was greeted by shrugs from the opposing team and moans of frustration from his own. Bobby blew them off, knowing he had no choice. Couldn't just leave the kid sitting there. There was something just not right about it.

None of the kids paid any attention to the man and dog sitting under a tree, sufficiently away from the game so as not to provide an obstacle.

The man's hair was brown, streaked with red. It was his latest color. He'd grown in a full beard again as part of his continuing effort to alter his appearance whenever possible. He had a high forehead, and his beard disguised the strong shape of his jaw. His steady, piercing gaze moved quickly and constantly, taking in everything. He wore a red down jacket and sat leaning against the tree, his legs pulled up in a vaguely fetal position.

He stroked the disguising beard in admiration and then glanced down at his companion. He tried not to laugh and outwardly didn't. Inwardly, he did, and the dog picked up on it.

What's so damned funny? demanded the dog. His voice sounded inside the man's head.

As was his habit, the man responded out loud, albeit softly. "I was just thinking how silly it is, me going to all the trouble of disguising my appearance, when I'm traveling with an animal as big as a bus."

No sillier than humans ever are, the dog informed him.

He reached down and patted the great canine on the back. "Dog" seemed an inadequate word to describe his companion, much as "car" did not begin to cover the machine that was parked at the roadside thirty yards away.

The dog was indeed the size to which the man had alluded. Not quite a bus, really. More the size of a horse. The creature was a German shepherd, brown with black spots, and a curious "Z" pattern etched in the fur on his forehead. It was this odd mark that had prompted the man to name him—through a rather torturous chain of logic that the dog still didn't understand—Rommel.

He talked with Rommel.

Not the way that people talk to a dog when they are giving instructions. There was no "Stand up," "Sit down," "Fetch the stick," et cetera, between the man and Rommel. They had full-fledged conversations, albeit they usually centered around eating, defecating, or humping since those were the dog's main areas of interest. Politics, theology, economics—these were not big on Rommel's topic list.

Rommel was telepathic.

So was the man.

The man's name was Chuck Simon. Whereas Chuck had chosen Rommel's name, Rommel had, of course, not chosen Chuck's. He had absolutely no interest in Chuck's name, quite reasonably pointing out that names were pointless between them since there was no one else that either of them would be talking to when they communicated with each other.

However, whereas Rommel was not interested in Chuck's name, there were many others who were greatly interested in Chuck's name. People from top covert organizations such as the Complex; people from the president's office; people from the Army. Chuck was a popular guy, so popular that he was wanted in all fifty-one states in the United States.

At that moment, Chuck wasn't interested in his name,

either. Or, for that matter, in all the people who would have liked to see him blown up, shot up, or nailed up. Chuck was instead interested in the small boy who had gotten into the game by default.

As a gym teacher he had seen the scenario enacted far too many times to make him comfortable. Why was it that there was always one kid who was the odd man out? He'd never encountered a social group of kids where absolutely everyone was popular. Rather it seemed that there always had to be one kid on whom everyone else dumped. It almost seemed that if such a kid didn't exist, it was necessary to invent him for the purpose of bias.

"Rommel, look at that poor kid," said Chuck.

Why? Does he have food on him?

Chuck shook his head. "I fed you a few hours ago."

Did you? I don't remember. Hunger makes me forget things.

Ignoring the comments of his dog with the bottomless pit of a stomach, Chuck watched the game unfold. It was not a pretty game, or an elegant game, but it was typical. The game was touch football, which suited Chuck just fine. He hated to see kids so young—or kids of any age—playing tackle football without any equipment on. They would get into their huddles, and Chuck remembered with amusement what such huddles were like. No professional calling of plays here. Instead the quarterback would briskly say, "You go here, you go over here, you go out there and come back," and so on.

And the littlest boy was having a tough time of it. It was clear that he was being given no specific instructions, because he would wander about aimlessly whenever his team was on offense. When he was on defense it was even worse. At first he had tried being on the line and rushing, but that had been even more hopeless. Touch football didn't mean no roughness at all, and the defensive guards would laugh off the kid's every attempt to make headway. Finally he gave up and instead worked on covering receivers. He double-teamed on the slowest moving of the receivers, but even in those cases he had trouble keeping up.

Chuck's heart went out to the kid . . . Paulie, he heard someone call him (accompanied by "you idiot," because Paulie had just gotten in the way and the man providing coverage had tripped over him).

"He's a gamer," said Chuck, watching the boy trudge back to the team as they prepared another defensive run.

"Look at him. They keep ignoring him, running over him—he still keeps at it."

Maybe he's just stupid.

"Or he's got real guts. Kid like that should succeed once in a while, don't you think?"

Rommel didn't even glance at him. *You have an idea, don't you?*

"Yes."

Does it involve food?

"No."

Then keep it to yourself.

Chuck half smiled and decided to wait for the next opportunity.

It presented itself on the very next play. The teams were evenly matched, and with all the scuffling, pushing, shoving, and so forth, no one had scored yet. Paulie took his position several yards in front of the line of scrimmage with a look of bleak, but hopeful, desperation on his face.

The center stood sideways. Boys that age felt creepy about the thought of reaching between each other's legs, so the center always snapped it sideways to the quarterback. The quarterback, a burly kid for a ten-year-old, briskly called out numbers that had no meaning to him or anyone else, but he did it because he knew the professionals did. He paused a moment to shove a hank of brown hair out of his eyes, and then yelled, in his high-pitched voice, "Hike!"

The center tossed the ball to him and started to push

his way through the crowd as the rushing line counted, "One miss'ippi, two miss'ippi," as fast as they could up to the required "five miss'ippi," wherein they would then attempt to rush the quarterback.

The quarterback fumbled the ball slightly, then recovered and backpedaled, looking for an opening.

Paulie ran in a small circle, and then was suddenly knocked over as Jimmy DelVecchi quickly cut right, eluding the man covering him. Paulie scrambled to his feet and set off in pursuit, as did the man who was supposed to be covering. They quickly outdistanced him as Paulie fell behind them by about ten feet.

Jimmy DelVecchi pulled slightly ahead of his cover, turned, and shouted, "Here! Here!"

The quarterback spotted him just as the rushers made it to "Five miss'ippi," drew back his arm, and uncorked a fairly impressive pass.

It spiraled through the air and Chuck actually took a moment to admire it. The kid had a good arm, maybe even a future. A future that would not be destroyed, certainly, by what was about to happen.

The gracefully spinning ball suddenly arced downward, a good twenty feet short of its goal, as if it had slammed into an unexpected headwind.

Someone, maybe it was Robert, shouted a warning, and Paulie looked up. He was alarmed to see the ball heading right toward him. He backed up a step and threw his arms up, partially in a doubtlessly hopeless effort to catch the ball, and partially to ward it off.

He braced himself, expecting it to hit him with a serious impact. Instead the ball settled into his arms with surprising smoothness.

He had the ball.

He had the ball. He looked at it in amazement, as if the ball had a mind of its own and had, in its wisdom, chosen him. Him!

Someone was screaming, "Run!" It was Robert. It was—

He heard the sounds of feet pounding after him and suddenly the full reality hit him. He hadn't just caught the ball. He had intercepted, which was really good. And maybe he could even score a touchdown, which was even better.

He started to run, his small legs churning up dirt.

There was nobody from his team near enough to run interference, although they were running toward him as fast as they could. Jimmy DelVecchi was right after him, his hands stretching out to grab him . . . and, he thought privately, shove him down hard, headfirst into the dirt, because the little creep had intercepted a pass meant for him . . .

Jimmy fell. He had no idea what tripped him up, but suddenly his legs went out from under him and he fell flat on his face.

Paulie kept moving. He dodged right and left, and kids who were pursuing him, for reasons they couldn't understand, were not able to catch up with him. They slowed, or they fell, and at one point Paulie seemed actually to leap about five feet to get out of the way of one pursuer. He soared through the air like a gazelle.

He kept on running and suddenly a cheer went up. He turned and saw that, without even realizing, he'd crossed the imaginary line. *Touchdown!* Just like he'd seen the guys do on TV, he spiked the ball.

It bounced straight back up and hit him in the face and he staggered slightly, but since he had his back to the other kids, no one saw it except Chuck, who winced slightly.

"Whoops," said Chuck. "Should have stopped the ball from hitting him."

You did more than enough, Rommel informed him. *I don't understand. What's the purpose of what they were doing?*

"It's called football."

So?

"The purpose is to score a touchdown by carrying the ball into the opposing territory across the goal line."

Rommel stared at him. *Does anyone get fed because of it?*

"No," sighed Chuck.

Does anyone hump because of it?

Chuck considered that. "Well . . . it can lead to that . . . especially with the right cheerleaders, and if you're a pro there are always groupies . . . yes. I suppose people can hump as a result of football, although that's not the intended purpose."

Rommel made a noise deep in his throat and settled his head onto his paws. *At least it has some value. So your helping that kid catch his football and run away from the other kids—that's going to lead to humping?*

"Not immediately, no."

You're going to keep helping him until it does, then?

Rommel had a good point actually. He watched the kids clapping little Paulie, (who had been the beneficiary of Chuck's considerable telekinetic power) on the back and congratulating him. Then they started to line up in preparation for continued play, and Chuck was wondering whether he had landed himself a permanent gig as this kid's guardian angel. That wasn't what he'd intended at all, and he wondered it there was a graceful way to get out of it . . .

The Lord provided, as the gray skies that had been threatening all day opened up and heavy rain started to pour down.

The kids scrambled for cover, slipping and sliding in a field rapidly turning to mud. It looked like serious rain, too, not about to let up anytime soon.

Chuck smiled as he pulled his jacket up over his head and started to jog toward his car, Rommel on his heels. Here was the graceful out he'd been hoping for. Whatever the boy did in his future—even if he never caught another ball—he would always be able to look back on that moment in his fond childhood memories and be cheered by it. That a powerful psionic named Chuck Simon had nudged the ball toward him, and tripped kids up with the power of his mind, were trivial details that he never needed to know.

The powerful sports car known as the RAC 3000, Ultraflame model, sat serenely by the curbside. Its gleaming red paint wasn't even streaking in the dirty rain that pelted it. Chuck didn't know what was in the paint job that protected it, but he had a feeling that he was as likely to rust as the car was.

"It's me," he said, for he'd left the car on voice ID mode. He hadn't even known it had voice ID mode until the car had informed him of it at one point during the recent weeks. The door promptly unlatched and swung open and he started toward it.

Then the door slammed shut again before he could get in.

He rapped on the window and called out in annoyance, "Hey! Rac! What's your problem? Let us in!"

The car said something, but it was obscured by the rain that was increasing in intensity. "*What?*" he shouted.

Automatically the car increased volume, and now he could hear the polite but firm voice of Rac's computer brain emerging from the speaker. "Sensors indicate rain," Rac informed him. The voice was crisp and female. When he had first heard it, it had seemed almost pleasant. Now there was a no-nonsense tone about it, as if the car had become more confident in its ability to handle its owner. Which perhaps it had.

"Damned right sensors indicate rain!" shouted Chuck. He hadn't used to use profanity so easily, but these days it was becoming more and more frequent. "Don't you think you should do something about that!" He pulled futilely on the door handle.

"You're correct, Charles," said Rac with that formality that had become maddening.

The windshield wipers came on.

"Open the door!" shouted Chuck, and he slammed a fist against the window. He didn't know why he was doing it. The blasted thing was bulletproof.

"You're wet," Rac informed him.

"I know I'm wet! That's why I want to come in!"

"You'll ruin my upholstery."

Chuck's eyes widened incredulously. "What?!"

"You and Rommel will soak up and dirty my upholstery. Although my exterior is conditioned to handle most routine damage, my interior is standard. I prefer to have clean seats."

Chuck leaned against the door, shaking his head.

What's wrong? demanded Rommel. He looked even less thrilled than Chuck, with his thick fur now thoroughly matted down.

"The car won't let us in." Chuck couldn't even believe he was saying it.

Why not?

"It's worried we'll get the seats dirty."

How would it like claw marks on its side?

That seemed worth a shot. "Hey, Rac! How would you like claw marks on your side!"

Incredibly, Rac made a scolding *tsk* sound. "Now, Charles . . . claws can't hurt me."

He was regretting the day he had instructed the car to stop calling him Mr. Simon, but instead to address him by his first name. It had promptly chosen the more formal "Charles" rather than "Chuck," and nothing he had said had been able to dissuade it to do otherwise.

He was rapidly beginning to suspect that Wyatt Wonder, the warped genius who'd given him the car, had done some sort of tinkering with the computer chips that gave the thing its personality. Perhaps he simply wanted to have some laughs at Chuck's expense. Wyatt Wonder was, after all, the man who had rigged an electronic whoopie cushion under the President of the United States during the Great Man's speech less than a month ago. The device had projected rude sounds of excessive flatulence directly into the television feed. At least, Chuck was certain that Wyatt was behind it. Wyatt had not openly taken credit for it, doubtlessly not wishing to detract from the worldwide headlines declaring that the President of the United States either had some sort of terminal digestive problem or was oblivious of his own body.

So would Wyatt Wonder, whose clandestine activities had already inspired an underground gag thriller called *The President's Plane Is Farting* that was making the rounds at college campuses, be above having a little fun at the expense of Chuck Simon?

The question did not seem to require an answer.

Chuck, water running down into his eyes, squinted and said, "It says claws can't hurt it."

Rommel promptly tested that by lifting his massive forelegs up onto the car and raking his claws across it. It made an earsplitting screeching noise, but there was no visible trail left behind on it.

"You'll have to stay out until the rain stops, Charles," the car told him, and with that formal "Charles" sounded more and more like Miss Spinoza, the sadistic first-grade teacher whose very name conjured up nervous shakes for Chuck. "Then dry off, and then you can get in."

Chuck drummed his fingers on the roof for a moment. "Now listen carefully," he said. "Are you listening?"

"Yes, Charles, I always listen to you," it said.

"Good. Now one of three things is going to happen in the next thirty seconds. Either I'm going to abandon you here, and you can stay here in all your pristine glory until someone comes along to tow you away to the impound lot. Or I might just use my TK power to blast open your window, because if you think being bulletproof is going to protect you against a TK bolt, you are sadly mistaken. Or you're going to open the door. Now choose."

The car appeared to consider it for a moment.

The door swung open and hit Chuck in the leg. He grunted from the impact.

"That . . . wasn't necessary," he snapped.

Rommel climbed into the back, his bulk as always taking up the entire rear seat. Again the car made that distasteful *tsk* noise, and it said, "You didn't have to threaten, Charles."

He climbed into the front and the door slammed shut for him. "I didn't appreciate that, Rac," he told her.

"You have to promise to buy some Dirtgon at the next auto supply store we pass. That will remove whatever dirt and"—the car paused in clear annoyance—"dog hair might be left on my nice clean seats."

"Fine, fine," sighed Chuck.

You're taking orders from this thing now?

"Shut up, Rommel."

This was not turning out to be one of his better days. Still, a day when someone wasn't trying to kill him was generally a plus for him.

He started up the car, preferring once again to use the manual controls, even though the RAC 3000 could have started itself and, indeed, gone anywhere he said to.

He started forward, driving carefully through a large puddle of water in front of him. *Where are we going?* Rommel asked.

"San Francisco," said Chuck. "Always wanted to go there."

You mean you're not going to stay around and help that boy catch balls thrown at him for the rest of your life?

"The rest is up to him," said Chuck. "And I'm sorry if you think it's stupid, Rommel. The simple fact is, I happen to like kids. Some are tougher than others, but even the rotten ones are, to a great extent, whatever they've been shaped into by their parents. All adults have a responsibility to help kids wherever they can. Besides . . . I never met a kid I didn't like."

3

There was a general perception among adults that private schools were somehow inherently superior to public schools. That the "riffraff" attended the latter, whereas clean-cut, devoted, and hardworking future leaders of America attended the former.

The fact of the matter was that at Golden Gate Academy, the most exclusive of the exclusive schools, situated high atop one of the many dizzying streets that had made San Francisco famous . . . there at Golden Gate, the kids could be as rotten as at any of the other schools.

For example, Matthew Olivetti might as well have been in attendance at one of the worst schools in the city, and he would just as easily have encountered the curious smell that was wafting from his gym locker.

Now it wasn't easy to separate that smell from the rest of the aromas of sweat and mildew that wafted through the boy's locker room. After all, they had just come in from their last workout before the Christmas break, which began the very next day. The coach had worked them especially hard, choosing to use the last day before vacation not as a graceful entry into a week off, but rather as a reminder that further torment and torture awaited them upon their return.

Like the other kids, teenage Matthew was covered with sweat, his T-shirt sticking to his hairless chest. Like the others, his muscles were sore and the air in his lungs seemed to sting as he tried to inhale it. Unlike the others, though, he wasn't moaning about it. He wasn't doing anything about it.

He was merely stoic, as always.

He was always stoic. After all these years, it had been deemed virtually impossible, by his peers, to get a rise out of him. His face was impassive and controlled. His round jaw was always set, his dark eyes glittering from apparently deep within his head. His jet-black hair was straight and hung down to just below his ears.

He was just a couple inches under six feet, and unlike other boys—whose ability to handle their body always seemed to lag behind the body's growth, making them seem a hopeless, jumbled tangle of arms and legs—Matthew always moved with the smoothness of glass.

When he spoke it was with almost sullen reluctance. But that did not mean that he was inattentive. His piercing gaze was frequently roving, taking in everything down to the minutest detail. Someone had once muttered under their breath that Olivetti acted as if he were sizing up the world for his intended future purchase of it. They had spoken under their breath, and had been certain that Olivetti hadn't heard them.

He had.

The next day a tree had inexplicably fallen over on top of the young quipster, and he'd been in the hospital for a month. No one had connected the bizarre accident with an off-the-cuff remark uttered about Matthew Olivetti the day before. Even if they had, it probably would not have made much difference.

That was three years ago, which to most teenagers is the equivalent of forever. Certainly Matthew had long since forgotten it, moving on to other and greater concerns. The most immediate was the nature of the smell in his locker.

He noticed that other kids who had already stripped to go shower were not moving quite as fast as they usually did. They were instead hovering nearby, trying to glance over their shoulders without being obvious, and so naturally were even more obvious than ever. There was some low chortling, an elbow in the ribs here and a "watch this" there.

Idiots.

He opened the locker and a dead rat tumbled out, plopping onto the wet tiled floor like an ugly dropping.

Matthew wasn't entirely sure what the kids had expected, and maybe they weren't sure themselves. They knew what they were hoping for—that Matthew would jump back in surprise, or give out some sort of alarmed yelp. Something to jolt him out of the constant, steady, and never-changing unflappability that the other kids found so irritating.

Matthew had never been popular. That was to be expected. And the kids had tried all kinds of stunts to display their utter contempt for him—a contempt that Matthew had been quite content to return.

He prodded the dead animal with his sneakered toe, staring down at it with clinical detachment. Then, without so much as a shrug, he began to undress.

He left the rat sitting there and was down to his jockstrap and socks when the coach showed up. Most of the other kids had already departed for the showers when Coach Kline stuck his head in and said, "What the hell is that stench around here? Somebody think they're the President of the United—jeez!"

He stopped, momentarily repulsed by the sight of the rat on the ground. It was the sort of reaction the kids had hoped to get from Matthew, and for which they had been most disappointed.

Since it was lying in front of Olivetti's locker, Kline promptly addressed the young man. "Olivetti! What the hell is that thing doing there!"

Matthew had finished undressing and had wrapped a towel around his middle. "Stinking, sir." Then, without another word, he walked away, leaving a sputtering Kline to get a broom and dustpan and pick the thing up.

Matthew walked to the showers and hung his towel in the drying room just outside it. In reality, the drying room was only marginally drier than the showers inside. He heard the other boys in there, laughing and snickering, the sounds of their voices echoing off the tiled walls.

Then he heard one voice, off toward the end, uttering a quick question, saying "Did he see what I put in there?"

He knew the voice immediately. Irvin. Gil Irvin. The guy who had, on several other opportunities, tried to embarrass or humiliate Matthew in public. In the past the attempts had always been abortive, or just too flat-out childish for Matthew to pay any attention.

This time, though—this time, Matthew was annoyed. Genuinely annoyed. Because Matthew had, if not a fetish, certainly a concern for The Way Things Should Be that extended beyond the normal parameters of someone who was seventeen going on eighteen. And part of that concern was that if something died, it should immediately be returned to the earth so it can be restored to the food chain. Death was not something to be treated lightly, or be taken as a practical joke.

Death was a serious business. Matthew knew that, since to him, the lives of other humans were his to take if he so desired. That was a great responsibility. He could not, would not, shirk it.

Would he take Gil's life?

He stepped into the large shower room, which had ten perpetually running showerheads lining either side. The chatter had grown momentarily quiet upon his entrance, as usually happened when the topic of conversation entered a room.

He lathered up, still mulling over the possible removal of Gil's life. From five showerheads over, Gil called over in that annoying nasal voice of his, "Got plans for the Christmas vacation, Matthew?"

Matthew said nothing for a moment, and then smiled thinly and remarked, "I figured I'm going to be busy. Shoveling."

"Shoveling what? Shit?" laughed Gil at his own unfunny remark.

"Snow," said Matthew. "Didn't you hear the weather report? It's going to snow. We're having a white Christmas this year."

Now the half-dozen boys left in the shower room made no effort to hide their laughter, and Gil was the loudest of all. "Snow? In California? In San Francisco? No way, man."

"At least six inches."

"That's four inches more than you'll ever be, dickhead," snorted Gil.

Matthew nodded to himself. "Care to bet on it?"

"What?"

"Bet. Money. I got a hundred says we have heavy snow."

Gil stepped completely under the shower, letting it roll off his head and slick down his hair. "You are fucking nuts," he said.

"I got a hundred."

"Why not a thousand?"

"Because you haven't got a thousand."

"Hey," said Gil with a shrug, "it's your money. You want to lose it, that's fine with me."

There was something wrong, and Bill Tyler, a muscular youth with flaming red hair, who was Gil's best friend, knew it. He wasn't sure what, but there was definitely something.

Gil and Bill went back a long ways. They went back so far that sometimes they were referred to as the "rhyming couplet," which prompted both of them to be major league womanizers to make sure no rumors started. Still, Gil and Bill were best of friends. Gil was the brains, Bill the brawn. But there was something warning brawny Bill this time that Gil wasn't using his brains.

"Don't do it, Gil," he warned him, without knowing why.

"C'mon, man, this guy wants to lose money that bad, I'm gonna take it from him," retorted Gil, soaping under his arms.

Matthew, meantime, had decided to let Gil live. He had reason to. He couldn't collect a bet from Gil if Gil was dead.

Still—he could teach him a lesson. The money wasn't enough. Gil had it coming, and had had it coming for a long time.

Gil's back had been to the water. Now he turned to face it, and it cascaded down his front—

—and went to boiling in an instant.

There had been no warning whatsoever, but suddenly the steady patter of the shower had become a deadly hiss, and steam billowed up.

Gil shrieked as the water went past boiling and rained down on him. His reaction had been automatic as he tried to leap back, but he slipped and went down. The water continued to pour on him, and he screamed and twisted and howled.

Bill tried to reach for him, but the pure intensity of the heat drove him back. Gil writhed on the ground and tried to pull himself away, scuttling like a crab. The water followed him, arcing impossibly after him like his own personal death-dealing rain cloud.

Kids were running everywhere, shouting for the coach,

screaming for help, because naturally they were afraid that the showers would turn on them next. They slipped and fell over each other to get out.

All except Matthew, who finished his shower calmly, ignoring the shouting around him and Gil's shrieks for help.

Gil tried to stagger to his feet but then he stumbled, his legs losing their strength, numb beyond the ability to feel pain. He slammed his head against the wall on the opposite side, fell to the ground, and, mercifully, passed out. The water continued to cook him.

Bill ran back in, his towel draped over his arm for protection, and he grabbed Gil's outstretched arm. A few drops of scalding water pelted him and he screamed, but he held on and dragged Gil out of the torrent of boiling water.

He kneeled over his friend, shouting Gil's name, and then looked up to see Matthew calmly emerge from the shower room. Matthew looked down, toweling off his hair, and shook his head. "Pity," he said, and walked right on past.

The ambulance had pulled up to the front of the school, and a large crowd of kids had gathered, ignoring the vice principal's obviously absurd statement that there was nothing to see here, and so they should move along.

They brought Gil out on a stretcher and there were gasps from the kids. He looked like a cooked lobster, his skin beet red and already blistering. He was scalded from head to toe.

The paramedics were about to load him into the van, and then something soft and cooling fell onto Gil's face. On the outskirts of consciousness, Gil felt it and heard the gasps of his classmates as more such coolness descended on him.

He forced his eyelids open and looked up.

It was snowing.

He caught a quick glimpse of Matthew standing at curbside. He had obviously dressed in a hurry, because his hair was still wet. The last thing he saw before he was slid into the ambulance was Matthew sticking his tongue out, catching snowflakes on his tongue.

4

Alex Romanova looked out the window in amazement.

It was snowing.

Certainly that was not an uncommon sight in Russia—in fact, back home it seemed more uncommon when it was not snowing.

But this . . . this was crazy.

There was a knock at the door.

Alex turned slowly. No one was expected. No one should be here. Alex pulled out a small but deadly pistol and called out, "Who's there?"

No response . . . except for a small noise, a scraping noise of paper.

An envelope was slid under the door, and Alex heard footsteps of someone quickly walking away.

It was a flat yellow envelope, with something stiff inside giving it support. Alex quickly opened the top and slid out several eight-by-ten photographs. A quick inspection revealed that they were all of the same person, a man with a fairly pleasant, but nevertheless somewhat hunted, expression. The pictures had been taken at a variety of locations, and the man had been changing his hair color or growing or shaving facial hair to try and disguise himself.

The phone rang, and Alex promptly picked it up.

"Those pictures," came the voice of Genady Korsakov, "are of Chuck Simon."

The name immediately rang a bell. "The renegade Complex agent? The one they call 'Psi-Man'?"

"Yes. We believe he's in or around the San Francisco area. Perhaps you can make use of him in the Olivetti business."

"What if he has no wish to get involved."

"If there's one thing that we have noticed, Alex, it's that Mr. Simon seems to have a positive knack for getting involved," observed Korsakov.

"You think he can handle Olivetti?"

There was a pause again. "I do not know," admitted Korsakov. "But I think, Romanova, that if you are fortunate enough to cross paths with Simon, that you may want to enlist him in any way you can. We have been keeping ourselves apprised of his activities, and I believe now may be the time to make some sort of move."

"What would you suggest?"

"That you use your wits. And that you be very, very careful."

"Thank you," said Romanova dryly. "And if I am not very careful?"

"Then you may be very, very dead."

There was a click at the other end.

Romanova had always thought that it was only in the cinema or on television that people stared at phone receivers after the other person had hung up. Which did nothing to explain why Alex sat and stared at the receiver for long minutes after Korsakov had gone on to other business.

• • •

Matthew hadn't expected to be accosted after school. Not that it surprised him all that much. It's just that it hadn't occurred to him that anyone would be that stupid.

The snow had already accumulated an inch, and he had decided that he was going to let it collect maybe another inch or two. He was three blocks away from home when someone stepped out of an alleyway, blocking his path.

Matthew said nothing for a moment, merely lifting an inquiring eyebrow.

"What do you want?" he asked finally.

Bill loomed over him, his fiery red hair dotted with flakes of snow. He had an unlit cigarette dangling out of his mouth. His jacket, much too light for the unseasonal chill of the air, was bunched around his shoulders.

"What'd you do to him?" whispered Bill. The snow was falling, creating an unnatural hush throughout a city that was very unaccustomed to such things.

He wanted to simply walk away, or walk around him. Or act dumb, or look at him with large, innocent eyes. So many bland things he could have said . . .

But why? What was the point? Here was the fact—he could say anything he wanted, and no one would listen to this thick-brained flunky of Gil's.

Matthew had been acting coy for as long as he could remember. He had been content to let the knowledge of his abilities rest within him. But he was going to be eighteen years old within a week. He knew what he was, and who he was. About time that the rest of the useless world knew it. Yes, and even better than that. Knew it . . . and couldn't do a damned thing about it.

Interesting, he thought. That this dunce would, in his simple, feebleminded way, be the one who got a real glimmering of what was going on. People far smarter than poor old Bill always chalked matters up to coincidence or happenstance.

"What did I do?" said Matthew. "That's easy. I scalded your buddy. Broiled him."

Bill's jaw dropped, and he snatched quickly at the cigarette that started to fall from his mouth. Clearly he hadn't expected such a blunt answer. Well, what had he expected? Nonsensical pussyfooting around? Where was the point in that?

Now Matthew could practically feel the confidence radiating from Bill. It was clear what was going through his pathetic little mind. He thought that Matthew was so scared of him that he was too frightened even to lie. That was rich. That was really rich.

But now that Matthew had shown clearly that he was afraid (or so Bill thought), Bill's confidence grew proportionately. He took out a cigarette lighter and, bringing up one hand, shielded it from the breeze as he lit it. "You realize I'm going to beat the shit out of you for that," Bill informed him.

"I don't think so," Matthew replied as Bill brought the lighter up to the cigarette.

The problem, Matthew realized, was that Bill was unaware of what precisely Matthew had done. Bill thought that Matthew had somehow rigged the showerhead through some mundane means. The truth, the simple truth, hadn't yet occurred to Bill. He thought that without any tricks to help him, Matthew would be easy pickings for him. That he would be able to, at will, pound Matthew into the ground.

He didn't understand that Matthew brought his tricks with him wherever he went.

The flame from the cigarette lighter leaped upward and enveloped Bill's head. His fiery red hair was on fire.

Bill screamed and started hitting at himself to try to put it out. It didn't help. The fire, with a life of its own, spread to the rest of his body with supernatural speed. Within seconds, Bill was a human bonfire.

Some vague recollection fought its way through the

haze of agony—a recollection of what one is supposed to do in such situations. Bill dropped to the ground and started rolling. The snow melted with a hiss, and Bill's skin was melting too with an equally loud hiss and a crackling noise, and a nauseating smell of charred meat.

Matthew Olivetti nodded briskly and walked around the burning body of Bill Tyler. The street was deserted, for this was a fairly exclusive neighborhood, so Bill should have plenty of time to be charbroiled before anyone found him.

And suddenly Matthew staggered, just as he got to the door of his house. Something, someone, had just . . . what? Just brushed against his mind. As if aware that he was around, that he had done something.

He was being watched. Or tracked. Or . . . what? What what what, dammit!

He threw open the door, staggered in, and then swung the door shut most of the way. He continued to peer out the crack though, watching the crackling, unmoving mass of what was certain to be the soon-to-be-late Bill Tyler.

A gleaming red car roared up.

It skidded to a halt in the snow, and someone got out. A man with a cap pulled down, and a dog—good Lord! The dog was getting out of the car, and he was almost as big *as* the car! The dog was looking around, and the man had unclipped something from underneath the dashboard of the car.

It was a fire extinguisher. He turned it on the blazing form of Bill Tyler and white foam poured out, covering him. Within moments he'd managed to get the fire out and then he quickly loaded the boy, or what was left of him, into the car.

The dog looked directly in Matthew's direction.

Matthew quickly closed the door and realized that his heart was pounding. He reestablished his customary control, fought for balance and the stoicism that had been part of him for so long.

Finally he risked a glance out the window, but the car was gone. And already the snow was covering over the charred place where Bill Tyler had been turned into a human barbecue.

"Good riddance," said Matthew Olivetti, and went on about his business.

5

Chuck had been cruising along the streets, trying to find just the right place for them to stay. Certainly a luxury hotel would be out of the question—the man with the huge dog would provide something of a curiosity to the staff, and it might even bring about the kinds of questions that could lead to uncomfortable answers.

But he didn't want to stay in a dump. He was getting a permanent kink in his back from sleeping in the car. He deserved a night or two in something better. So did Rommel. So, for that matter, did Rac, who complained ceaselessly that they were mussing up her (its, dammit!) interior. So if he was going to stay in a hotel or motel, as his present frame of mind was inclining him to do, it wasn't going to be one with paper-thin walls and rats the size of his grandmother.

Funds would not be a problem. In the glove compartment, he had found one more parting gift from Wyatt Wonder: an assortment of Cards.

The Card was the one absolute necessity one needed in

the world these days. You were issued a Card at birth, and everyone carried one for their entire life. It served as an all-purpose identification, and also deducted credit from an ongoing account for any purchase. Salary money and the like was paid directly into the credit account, and so the need for any actual cash to change hands had gone completely by the wayside.

Using his personalized Card, though, was not an option for Chuck. He'd be so traceable that the Complex would be on him inside of an hour after he'd used it. Then he would be dragged back, kicking and screaming, to their headquarters, where a simple lobotomy would turn him into a cheerful and willing psychic assassin, wiping out the bad guys in the name of the government of these United States. A government that had done away with the Bill of Rights years ago. At the time the president had cheerfully declared, "No one'll miss 'em anyway. Most people can only quote the first and fifth one anyways, and the first one lets you burn flags, and the fifth one lets criminals refuse to talk. Who needs this shit?"

And the American people, who had never had to fight for the rights handed to them at birth, didn't know how to fight to stop them from being taken away. So they didn't, and they were.

False ID Cards were tough to come by. Unless, of course, you were master showman and genius Wyatt Wonder. Then you could pull off little miracles such as providing valued allies with a variety of fake IDs. Doubtlessly Wyatt himself was tracking them, though. It was his way of keeping tabs on Chuck, in the event he needed the Psi-Man at some point in the future. Well, Chuck was willing to concede that. It was a small point indeed considering that it now gave him some room with which to maneuver in the world that oftentimes seemed far too small to . . .

That was when his senses went mad all around him.

Chuck gasped and completely lost control of the wheel.

He slid to one side and banged his head against the passenger side door, all the time moaning and clutching at his head.

In the back seat, Rommel had gone berserk. His bark was a roar like a cascading waterfall, and Chuck didn't know where to think or concentrate first.

Rac reacted within a second. The car only had time to slide a foot or two before the on-board computer took over, overriding manual control.

Rac promptly straightened her wheels and guided them forward. The car ceased its skidding and made the first convenient pull over to a curb. The car's engine idled as Rac shifted into park.

Immediately Chuck was sitting up. "Go!" he gasped out. "Up ahead! That way!"

"What is the problem, Charles?" asked Rac politely.

"That way!" It was everything he had not to pass out. He gripped the steering wheel and shoved the gear into drive.

"Charles, I do not think you are in any condition to—"

"Drive, blast it!" He slammed on the gas, and Rac had no choice but to proceed as instructed.

What was it? demanded Rommel.

"I don't know," said Chuck, "but it's up this way."

Great. Then let's go back the other way.

"We have to see what happened!"

No, you have to see. You and that strange belief that everyone's problem is yours. I don't have to see. I have to get out. This will get me nothing but trouble.

In his heart, Chuck knew Rommel was right. He really was transporting the animal against his will, purely because Chuck's beliefs as a Quaker made him unable to simply turn away when he witnessed or knew of trouble.

And there was definitely trouble. One of the side abilities of Chuck's psionic power was being able to detect when there was major trouble around—usually trouble caused by someone with psionic abilities. It had given him timely warning in more than one instance and saved him from ambush.

This time, though, he knew—he didn't know how he knew, but he did—that there was more than danger ahead. He knew that he was needed, that someone was suffering at the hands of . . .

At the hands of what?

He didn't know, except that whatever it was was just up ahead and around the corner.

He spun the wheel and the car skidded for a moment, unaccustomed to maneuvering on something as un-Californian as snow. Then, even as Chuck regained control, he saw it.

Someone was on fire.

Only twice before had he seen something remotely resembling that—when, at a friend's house, his friend's father had accidentally set himself on fire while lighting one of those old, illegal charcoal briquette-burning barbecues. The other time . . . had been because of his losing control of his power, and he didn't like to think about that.

What he was seeing was like those safety films he used to make the kids watch, back in the simple, calm days when he was a high school coach, whose greatest ambition in life was to teach history rather than make history.

The car skidded to a halt and Chuck leaped out. Rommel was right behind him. Inwardly, Chuck was pleased to note that once Chuck had made the decision, Rommel had backed him up one hundred percent without any further comment.

He saw the burning boy and tried to think quickly of the best way to proceed, blotting out the sheer horror of it. That was when Rac said politely, "You are aware that there is a fire extinguisher situated beneath my glove compartment."

No. He hadn't known. Duh.

He grabbed it and turned it on the boy, who had stopped shrieking and, for all Chuck knew, might be dead.

Rommel, in the meantime, turned slowly in a circle, his head held high, as if sniffing the air. This would have been an incorrect perception. He wasn't sniffing it so much as sensing it.

It's around here, he said. *Or at least it was.*

"What was it?"

I don't know. Nasty.

Someone or something had caused this horror to occur. Chuck wasn't sure what it could have been, but the thought of someone just lighting this kid up was terrifying. Nasty, as Rommel had put it.

He knew that, technically, he shouldn't be moving the boy at all. That he should wait for an ambulance. But he had the certain feeling that the kid wasn't going to be able to last that long. So he picked the boy up, trying not to think about what he was touching.

Then he realized that he didn't have to. Using his TK power, he elevated the boy just slightly above his own arms. To any casual onlooker, it would appear as if he were carrying him when, in fact, he was hovering about a half inch above Chuck's arm. He wasn't quite sure who would be a "casual onlooker" to such a horrible happenstance, but there were ghouls everywhere, he supposed.

He got back to the car and slid the boy in as Rommel continued looking around. The dog was annoyed. He should have been able to lock it down. It was as if whatever had caused all this had somehow managed to cloak its presence. That was an extremely disturbing thought, and Rommel growled softly in frustration.

"Rommel! Come on!"

Making a last quick check and coming up empty, Rommel followed Chuck into the car.

"Rac," said Chuck briskly, "target the nearest hospital."

The car had comprehensive maps of most major cities in its computer bank. On a small screen situated in the middle of the dashboard, a glowing road map of San Francisco snapped into existence. Inside of a moment, a small glowing spot appeared. "There it is, Charles," Rac told him.

"Take us there."

You're letting the car drive?

"It can get us there faster than my having to navigate through strange streets."

Let me out.

"Be quiet, Rommel."

The car rolled away from the curb and shot toward the hospital, leaving a smeared spot of melted snow and foam on the ground.

The waiting area was not an elaborate affair. A couple of prints of ducks and flowers were bolted to the pale green wall. The carpet was threadbare and needed to be replaced, and the few sticks of furniture had plastic over the upholstery. Rommel lay on the floor, his muzzle on his paws, as Chuck drummed on the chair he was seated on.

Let's just go.

"Not until we find out what the story is with the boy," Chuck replied stubbornly.

We did our good deed.

Chuck knew that. Technically, he even knew that, on the surface of it, there really was no reason that they had to hang around.

Except there was. Something had caused that to happen to that boy, and he wanted to be able to talk to the boy and learn what it was.

He stood as the doctor entered. He was a short man with graying hair and a fraying air. "You're the man who brought that boy in?" asked the doctor. "The burn victim?"

"Yes, that's right. How is h—"

"We did all we could. I'm sorry."

Chuck's face fell. "He's . . . he's dead?"

"I'm afraid so."

Chuck sagged back down into the chair. "God . . . I shouldn't have moved him. I . . ."

"Technically, you're right," said the doctor briskly, but not unkindly. "Frankly, though, I don't see where it would have made much difference. It was shock as much as anything else." He shook his head. "Damned strange is what it is. Second boy from that school in the same day. Damned strange."

Chuck had had his hands in his face. Now he looked up, curious. "What school?"

"Golden Gate." He checked his pad. "We got a positive ID on the boy as one William Tyler. Senior at Golden Gate Academy on High Street. That's the second kid we've brought in for burns today. First one got roasted in a berserk shower, if that isn't the damndest thing."

"Is the other boy still here?"

He glanced at his pad once more. "Yes. Gil Irvin."

"Can I talk to him?"

"Are you a policeman or something?" The doctor had tucked the pad back under his arm and was peering over his glasses at Chuck.

"No. Just a concerned citizen."

"Really. A concerned citizen, Mr. . . . ?"

"Green. Chuck Green." It had been an easy name to remember, because he'd gotten it from the color of the wall. It was the name he'd given the police when they had questioned him upon his arrival at the hospital. These days there were always a couple of cops on duty at emergency wards, to be able to promptly start investigations in matters such as this one. The two cops who'd questioned him had clearly, at first, thought he might have something to do with the boy's condition. But Chuck's obvious condition of concern and his earnestness quickly dissuaded them from considering Chuck anything more than a simple passerby.

And now the doctor was saying, "Mr. Green, I appreciate your good citizenship, but you've done all you can. Go home."

"Any idea what caused him to just go up like that?" Chuck asked. "Was there gasoline on him or something?"

The doctor frowned. Clearly he wasn't sure why Chuck was so interested. "No. No trace of any chemical. Frankly, it's damned peculiar. I'm sure the coroner's report will tell us more. But you, sir, know all you need to know at this time."

With a clear indication that that was all that was going to be said, the doctor turned and walked out of the waiting room.

Chuck looked down at Rommel. "Wait here," he said briskly.

Why?

"No dogs allowed where I'm going."

Typical human lack of taste.

Chuck found a directory on the wall, and quickly made his way to the burn ward. He was determined to find the room that this Gil Irvin was staying in. Something—he wasn't sure what, but something—was telling him that there was more to this than just a simple freak accident. Something wrong. Something very sinister.

He walked past one room after another and then suddenly stopped as someone was wheeled out of a room on a gurney by two dour-looking orderlies. A sheet covered the body from head to toe, but Chuck had a feeling he knew.

"Is that Bill Tyler?"

One of the orderlies glanced at him. "It was," he said. They wheeled him away, the gurney squeaking softly and repeatedly.

Chuck stood there, watching the gurney dwindle, and then someone touched him on the arm.

He looked down.

It was a priest.

The priest came to about Chuck's shoulder. He had a mop of blond hair, and a craggy but concerned face. His nose was slightly too large for his head. When he spoke his voice was raspy, and sounded vaguely British.

"You brought that boy in?" he asked.

Chuck nodded. "That's right. You're his priest?"

The priest shook his head. "You work with the hospital, then?" Chuck said, and again the priest indicated no.

Chuck frowned. "Then who are you?"

"Father Pertwee," said the priest. "And you and I have to talk."

"We do?"

"Yes."

There was an almost demented urgency in the priest's voice. "What," asked Chuck, "do we have to talk about?"

The priest glanced right and left, as if terrified that they were being spied upon. There was a steady, throbbing sense of urgency about him. He lowered his voice and said, "Not here."

"Where then?"

"Pier 39. Tomorrow. Six P.M. It's a matter of life and death."

"Whose?"

"Everyone's." And without another word, the priest turned and walked away, leaving Chuck scratching his head in confusion.

He had wanted to make sure that Bill was dead.

As time had passed, Matthew Olivetti's poise and self-confidence eroded ever so slightly. What if Bill Tyler did manage to convince someone? What if people did listen to him? What if—a lot of things.

Matthew began to wonder if perhaps he hadn't acted precipitously. Sure, it had felt good, having good old Bill writhing in the grasp of his power. Good old Bill, not fully realizing what he was facing even as his brain was cooking.

It was making Matthew nervous. Nervous to the point of wondering if perhaps he shouldn't do something about it.

He called the nearest hospital, guessing that that was where Bill's mysterious savior would probably bring him. He asked about Bill's condition and was told that Bill was in critical condition.

Critical. That sounded good. Very promising. A condition from which if Bill happened to die, no one would be very surprised.

Matthew considered that to be his cue.

His parents were not home yet. This wasn't shocking. His mother was tied up with clients and his father was in London on business. The servants had the week off that, frankly, Matthew considered a bit expansive on his parents' part, even for Christmas week. Still, he could live with it if he had to. But Bill, and the prospect of him getting better—that was definitely not something he could live with. Or had to live with.

He cabbed over to the hospital and had to fight to suppress his glee when told that good old Bill had given up the ghost mere minutes before. Realistically that was all he needed to know. Now, though, morbid fascination drew him. He wanted to see the stiff, so he politely asked the nurse if he could pay last respects. The nurse told him to go away, and looked at him with a fair amount of distrust bordering on disgust.

So after being told that he couldn't go where he wanted, he went there anyway. He had generally found that when it came to places like hospitals, they counted far more heavily on forbidding signs, stern glances, and ingrained respect for authority than they did on security guards. This, of course, proved useless in Matthew's case since he had no respect for any authority other than his own.

He came up the stairs and was about to emerge when something held him back. He wasn't sure what—some sort of instinct, or internal warning. He peered through the crack of the door, acting clandestine for the second time that day, and his eyes opened wide. Instinctively, without even knowing how, he shielded his presence from someone who he didn't even consciously know could detect it.

There was that guy who had pulled up in the red car, standing right there in the hallway not ten feet away. Good old Bill's personal knight in shining armor. But who was he talking to?

A priest.

Matthew frowned. That priest looked familiar somehow. Where had he seen him before?

Everywhere.

Slowly it dawned on Matthew. He'd seen that priest around a lot of places. Except he wasn't always dressed as a priest.

Tumblers clicked in Matthew's mind. Yes. Definitely. He hadn't thought anything about it at the time, but the guy had been hanging around at the school a lot. Dressed shabbily, he'd always come across as just some sort of street bum or something. One of the regulars of life who are on the outskirts of one's awareness.

Who was this guy? And who was the other guy? Were they in it together? In what? What was going on?

He heard the priest mention something about Pier 39 tomorrow at 6 P.M. The priest then walked away down the corridor, leaving the man from the car looking very puzzled.

No. No, they weren't in together on whatever it was. Matthew was now definitely sure of that. So the question became, what was going on?

He went back down the stairs quickly, to try to catch up with the priest, hoping to head him off when he came out another exit. But after standing in the street for almost a quarter of an hour, Matthew came to the conclusion that he'd missed the priest.

All right then. Six P.M. tomorrow. He wouldn't miss him again.

6

Once upon a time, Pier 39 had been just one of the many piers that extended out from the area known as Fisherman's Wharf. And then, slowly, it had been built up as a major tourist attraction as more and more shops came in, appealing to a dazzling array of interests. There was everything from stuffed toys to cookies to places where you could buy pearl necklaces for loved ones by selecting and cracking open your own oyster.

In recent years, tourism had dropped off as seismic reports had become more and more vocal. The Big One—the devastating earthquake that was always believed to be the one that would virtually end life in California as it was known—was believed imminent. At some point very soon, the massive fault lines would deliver a blow to San Francisco and the surrounding areas that would be beyond all records on the Richter scale.

California tourist bureaus, as was their job, downplayed these predictions. They were successful to some degree, but not as much as they would have liked. A number of

stores along Pier 39 had already closed and not been re-
rented. It was anticipated that more would be closing
soon. Some of the vibrancy along the pier had been lost,
but there was still some hope for a turnaround.

Chuck and Rommel walked slowly down the pier,
glancing around with only mild interest. When one is constantly on the alert and scanning crowds for possible as-
sailants and ambushes, it's hard to relax and enjoy
something as trivial as a glorified shopping mall. But
Chuck was giving it his best effort. Rommel, who had
chowed down shortly before on a couple of raw steaks
picked up at a supermarket, was momentarily not griping
about his stomach. Chuck appreciated the respite.

What's that? inquired Rommel as they passed a partic-
ularly gaudy-looking building that had a line of people
waiting to get in.

Chuck glanced at the sign. "That's where they have a
show that simulates an earthquake. Like that big earthquake they had back in 2014, during the series between
the Giants and the Sox."

What? What series? What giants? What socks?

Chuck laughed softly. "They're baseball teams. The
San Jose Giants, the only team to be in two world series
that were interrupted by earthquakes. And the Boston Red
Sox."

Are the Giants tall?

"Not inhumanly, no."

Do the other men look like socks?

"Not at all."

*This is another stupid human thing, isn't it. Like names,
and commercials, and war.*

Chuck stepped aside to let a little boy run in pursuit of
a bouncing ball. "It's not stupid. It's exciting. There they
were, the seventh game of the World Series. The Sox were
over the Giants 11–0 in the second inning. It was incredible. Then this earthquake hit. The park was devastated,
and the dugout collapsed on the Sox. Most of the team

was killed or injured, and two months later when they finally replayed the seventh game, they had to start over since it wasn't official. The Sox—what remained of them, including a lot of kids called up from the minors—got clobbered by the Giants. Right after that they sold off the franchise. The owners said that they didn't want to continue dealing with a team that was so jinxed, even God didn't want them to win. Kinda depressing, actually. That's why the Sox now play in New Jersey."

Rommel stared at him. *You have a distorted sense of excitement, you know that?*

Chuck disdained to answer that remark. "At any rate," he said, "that building with all the people standing in line simulates an actual earthquake. It's like a show. You go in and they shake you up. Kind of like a tax audit."

And this is fun?

"Well, yes, I suppose."

So if there was a real earthquake, that would be even more fun.

"No, that wouldn't be fun at all."

Rommel glanced at the line. *So those people are waiting to experience something for fun that if it really happened, they'd be terrified.*

"That's basically correct."

You going to attempt to defend that?

"No," sighed Chuck. "If I couldn't explain football and baseball to you, I'm sure not going to bother with earthquake shows."

That's probably wise.

They walked some distance more, until they were approaching the end of the wharf. They stood outside a store that dealt exclusively in licensed merchandise from Wyatt Wonder—a chain of stores collectively called Wondermarts—and Chuck glanced around, his hands in his pockets. "I don't see the guy."

I don't even know what we're doing here.

"Waiting for that priest."

Why?

Chuck gave it some thought. "I don't know."

I could never be a human. I always know what I'm doing and why.

He scratched the great beast on the head, just above the odd Z-shaped symbol in his fur. "Don't worry, Rommel. If you were a human, you'd be just as screwed up as the rest of us."

Rommel actually seemed to shiver at that. *And you thought earthquakes were frightening.*

Chuck continued to look around. The salt air was sharp in his lungs and he walked over to look at the ocean lapping up around the pier. Slowly he shook his head. When he'd been living the simple, uncomplicated life of a gym coach in the middle of the country, he never thought he'd ever see an ocean. He thought he'd live out his life in simple obscurity. Never for a moment had he dreamed what turns his life would take. It was crazy. What was he doing here? What had happened to him? Every so often he still believed that he would just wake up one day in Ohio, blinking his eyes furiously against the light, and everything that had happened to him would fade away like a dream.

For that certainly had to be all it was. Homicidal government agents, telepathic dogs, talking cars—what the devil kind of life was this, anyway? Certainly nothing that could exist in any sort of real world.

He glanced at an empty carton of cigarettes that was sitting at his feet, discarded without so much as a thought to the awful condition the environment was already in. His mind lifted it into his hand and then he stared at it. Was his power that casual now? He supposed it was. If this was a dream, at least it was a consistent one.

There's someone coming up directly behind you, Rommel's voice spoke softly in his head. *Should I kill him?*

"You know the answer to that," Chuck said just as softly.

Just testing.

Chuck turned quickly, marshaling his TK power and holding it in check, like a coiled spring, ready to release it. In addition the muscles in his body prepared to go into action with the proven speed and mastery of physical combat that his aikido gave him. It had taken him only a second to be prepared, offensively and defensively, to face . . .

A priest.

Chuck partially relaxed his guard. "Ah, I was wondering when you would show up."

"I'm sorry," he said, glancing around. "I wanted to make sure I wasn't followed. He has remarkable powers, you know, and incredible resources."

"He? He who? Would you mind telling me what this is all about, Father . . . Pertwee, was it?"

He nodded distractedly, and looked out over the water. It lapped gently against the wharf, and the sky was already darkening. "When I was a boy, I loved the ocean. I loved to sit on a shore and stare across, and wonder if way on the other side, in some other country beyond my vision or understanding, there wasn't another boy looking back in my direction. That we might be staring at each other and never know. And I wondered about life beneath the sea, about the creatures that lived down there, swimming about. I wondered if they even knew we existed. And if they did know, did they care?"

Father Pertwee leaned against the railing. His heavy coat was drawn around him against the stiff breeze. The bizarre snowfall of the previous day had stopped for the moment, but befuddled weathermen were predicting that more would be dumped upon the puzzled inhabitants of San Francisco before the night was out. There was a chill in the air that Chuck might have found invigorating, were the whole scene not giving him the creeps.

"What's beneath the water, I would wonder," the priest said, as if unaware that Chuck was there anymore. "It was so dark, so foreboding, so . . . evil. There is a great deal of evil in the world, don't you think, Mr. . . . ?"

"Chuck Green," said Chuck Simon.

"Mr. Green." The priest scratched absently at his blond hair. "Do you think there's evil?"

Chuck, of course, knew firsthand about aspects of evil. But he sensed that there was more to the question. "You mean evil generated by man?"

The priest smiled thinly, as if pleased that Chuck had picked up on things unsaid. "Evil," he said, "as a force of nature. As solid as the earth, as powerful as the wind, as hot as flame, as deep as the ocean. Evil."

You want to fill me in here? asked Rommel.

Chuck didn't answer his dog. He couldn't. He wasn't entirely sure what to say. He had not known what to expect when this beleaguered, haunted-looking man had approached him in the hospital, but somehow this sure wasn't it.

"What are we talking about?" Chuck asked him.

The priest did not look back at him. "You brought in that boy, that poor unfortunate child. A lad who looked as if he'd been through the fires of hell itself, did he not?"

Chuck nodded. The priest had his back to him and didn't see the nod, but he didn't have to. "The fires of hell," continued the priest, "is a more apt metaphor than you know."

"Look"—Chuck's hands moved in a vague, dissatisfied fashion—"sir, with all due respect, I'd really love to stand here, talking all night about your boyhood recollections and the nature of evil and aquatic life and such. And naturally I was horrified by what happened to that boy. The doctors still don't know how it happened, and I wish—"

"What denomination are you?" It was as if the priest hadn't heard a word he said.

Chuck sighed. "I'm a member of the Society of Friends."

The priest looked at him with interest. "A Quaker.

Good people. Not much for clerical figures."

"No, sir."

"Still, a good people. Solid philosophies. One of them is about bearing witness, as I recall. That if you see something immoral or wrong occurring, that you simply can't turn your back and pretend it didn't happen. Is that right?"

"Something like that."

"And what are your personal thoughts on God?"

Chuck paused a moment, thinking about an old comic strip he'd seen reprinted in a collection. A small boy sitting under a tree, and some sort of cartoon tiger was next to him. And the tiger asked the boy, "Do you believe that there's a God?" And the boy replied, "Well, *someone* is out to get me."

In Chuck's case, he knew exactly who was out to get him, and sometimes it was a test of his faith that there could be a God who permitted such evil to exist in the world. A test, though, that he had not yet failed.

"Yes," he said slowly, "I believe that there's a God. Sometimes I wish he'd fill me in on what his game plan is."

"And do you believe in Satan?"

Rommel whined from nearby. He was getting bored. Chuck couldn't blame him. He let out a slow breath. "Sir," he said softly but firmly, "tell me what this is about, or I'm leaving. I can't put any finer a point on it than that."

The population on the wharf was thinning out considerably. Overhead Christmas lights had been strung, and the alternating flickering of green and red danced across the priest's face, making him look like some sort of religious traffic light.

"The devil," said the priest, "has a son."

Chuck raised an eyebrow. "I beg your pardon."

"The devil has a son." This time it was said with more conviction. "Just as our Lord had a son, so did the devil."

At this point Chuck was ready to turn and leave. What

in the hell was he doing here? The devil had a son? There was a devil, and he had a kid trotting around on earth? Absurd. Ridiculous.

What's going on? asked Rommel. *What's he talking about?*

Chuck was about to answer him, and then realized that the concept of a man responding to his talking dog precluded the possibility of Chuck being the one to call the kettle black. Still . . .

"The devil has a son," Chuck repeated, like a kind of warped mantra. "Let me guess. He's a Hollywood agent."

He thought the priest might start to scream at him for that, or slap him, or accuse him of blasphemy. The moment the priest did that, Chuck would turn and walk away and have done with this lunatic.

Instead the priest smiled. "That's very amusing, Mr. Green. Most amusing. I wish it were a laughing matter. I wish, frankly, that I were insane. That what you were listening to was the maunderings of a deranged individual. I must regret to inform you, however, that they are not."

Chuck steepled his fingers and walked in a small circle for a moment, composing his thoughts. Rommel stared at him, not sure what to make of any of this, Chuck's confusion mirrored in Rommel's own mind.

"So . . . so all right," said Chuck. "So I'm supposed to believe that there's a demonic child running around. And I'm to infer, from what you've said, that this . . . child . . . is responsible for what happened to that boy."

"That is correct."

"All right. So . . . why come to me?"

The priest's smile was positively angelic. "The Lord has told me to."

"I'm gone," said Chuck, and he started to walk away.

The priest came up quickly behind him and placed a strong hand—a surprisingly strong hand—on Chuck's forearm. From nearby Rommel growled warningly. If the priest heard the ominous noise of the dog, he made no indication of it. Instead he said simply, "Matthew Olivetti."

Chuck turned and looked at him. "Pardon?"

"The devil's son is named Matthew Olivetti," the priest said.

"Is he now."

"Yes."

"Doesn't sound like an especially threatening name."

"Perhaps. But he is a most threatening individual."

The priest walked back toward the water, as if he no longer cared whether or not Chuck stayed to listen anymore. This, naturally, was enough to prompt Chuck to remain where he was.

This was all nonsense. It had to be nonsense. "So this kid's parents . . . they are . . . ?"

"Lyle and Carol Olivetti," the priest told him. "Very successful people. Homes in New York, London, and here in San Francisco. His mother is a lawyer, his father an immensely successful real-estate man."

"And this Lyle and Carol . . . they're Mr. and Mrs. Satan, is that it?" He couldn't believe he was saying this out loud. He noticed some people casting him a strange look as they passed by. He couldn't blame them. If the situations were reversed, he'd do the same thing.

"No. They're both mortal . . . but Lyle is not the boy's true father. Satan came to Carol Olivetti and lay with her in her sleep to produce his spawn upon the earth."

Chuck wasn't sure which was more fantastic. That this guy was spouting all these things, or that Chuck was standing there listening to it. "Don't take this wrong," said Chuck, "but wasn't there an old movie about this?"

"Movies," said the priest. "Books, holo-vid programs, writings going back centuries predicting exactly when, where, and how the world would end." He turned to face Chuck. "Look around you, Mr. Green. See the world that we live in. A world thick with pollution and disease. A world where our government has gone from one of the most free to the most oppressive, in a far shorter time than anyone would have suspected possible. Haven't you wondered how such a thing was possible?"

"It happens," said Chuck. "Things happen. People don't appreciate the freedoms they have, and so they have none."

"No," said the priest vigorously. "Not that simple. And the coming of the anti-Christ . . . for make no mistake, that is exactly what he is . . . is the final step. What they have been waiting for. And they're waiting for him to come into his full strength and power."

"They?" Chuck was confused. "Who are—"

The priest hadn't heard him, or wasn't listening. He was speaking faster and faster, as if afraid that time was running out for him. "The boy, Matthew Olivetti, is soon to come into his full strength. His birthday, of course, is December 25. I'm sure you could have guessed that. And this week, this December 25, is the day that he will come into the full strength of his powers. They have been steadily growing over the years, and his moral sense has decayed. He has grown stronger and stronger, and more and more willing to use his powers to his own nefarious ends. This December 25 is when he will be at the age of power. He will turn eighteen."

"Why is eighteen the age of power?" asked Chuck, intrigued in spite of himself.

"Do you know the sign of the beast?"

Chuck frowned a moment. "Yeah . . . hold it . . . numbers, right? Right!" and he snapped his fingers. "Six six six. Oh, I get it. Six three times is eighteen. Okay. You've convinced me. Let's get a stake and drive it through him."

"Stop it!" said the priest with a surprising amount of fury. "Don't you think I know how this sounds? Don't you think I *know* that? The good Lord came to me six months ago and told me of the evil. He told me of Matthew Olivetti. In a world that believes in mundane matters, I've been touched by divinity, and I'm being asked to convince others of that. You have no idea what I'm going through. You have no idea how it is to be a sane man in a world of insanity, but that world believes that just the opposite is true. Listen to me, please! Six months ago, I went to a reporter. I told her my story, and she believed me . . ."

"A reporter believed you?" asked Chuck incredulously.

"Perhaps not fully," admitted Father Pertwee. "Perhaps not at all. But she started to do investigations, and found the trail of bodies left in the wake of Matthew Olivetti. Incidents that seemed random and unattached, unless you knew what to look for. If you don't believe me, talk to Carmen Friedman. She'll show you all the information that she has turned up. She'll convince you, even if I haven't been able to."

Can we leave now?

"Yes, I think so," Chuck said to Rommel.

"You think she will convince you?" said the priest hopefully.

Chuck sighed. It wouldn't do to tell the priest who Chuck had just addressed. The priest might think that Chuck was as crazy as he was.

He didn't know what to make of this nonsense at all. Chuck's ability didn't enable him to read thoughts, but he could certainly sense impressions. And the impression he was receiving from this man was that there was something being kept from him. That the priest wasn't being entirely truthful. On the other hand, the good father was definitely frightened. Something was upsetting him tremendously, and Chuck knew that it had to be this Matthew Olivetti kid.

The Satan spawn. The bringer of chaos.

Bull. It couldn't be. It just couldn't, that was all.

Chuck turned to walk away, and suddenly he was suffocating in feelings of danger.

He staggered, Rommel's furious barks sounding thick and far away. He spun, trying to lock down where it was

coming from. It was the same as before, when he had
found that burning boy . . .

Pier 39 began to rumble.

Let's get out of here! Rommel shouted in his mind.

All around him, people were screaming. The pier moved
under him, a terrifying feeling. The one thing people always counted on, always knew would be there, was the
ground beneath their feet and the sky over their head.
When the ground began to toss about, like a giant shrugging his shoulders, it so distorts one's worldview that one
half expected the sky to crash down.

And now the screams of the people were mingling with
a roar like the gates of hell being hurled open upon massive hinges. The pier shook violently, and Chuck was
hurled off his feet. Falling was nothing new for him—
he'd spent hours upon hours during aikido training doing
nothing but falling. Even now, with the earth buckling
under him, his old instincts took hold and he executed a
perfect roll, coming back up to his feet. He looked around
frantically for the priest, shouting his name.

He spotted the priest, over by the water, hanging on
desperately to the iron railings. The priest was screaming
something, over and over, and Chuck couldn't hear
what the frantic clergyman was saying. Then he lip-read
enough to make it out—

"It's him!" the priest was shouting. "It's him! It's him!"

Somewhere in the back of Chuck's mind, a sixth-grade
English teacher primly corrected, *"It is he,"* and then he
brushed that aside. He glanced in Rommel's direction.
The dog was having an easier time of it, balanced on the
far more efficient four legs than two. He looked back to
the priest and reached out with the power of his mind to
pull the priest away . . .

And suddenly a column of water smashed up through
the pier, just to Chuck's right, slamming him back with
the force of an anvil. It knocked the breath out of Chuck
and he gasped, clutching at his chest. He tried to scramble

to his feet, and water exploded just to his left. Water was geysering everywhere, the entire pier rumbling. People were running like mad, and the nice, cheery stores all around started crumbling, collapsing in on themselves like houses of cards.

Water cascaded down on Chuck, drenching him. He took in a lungful, coughed it up, and staggered around it, shielding his eyes and trying to locate the priest. He saw the priest, still clutching on to the railing for dear life and screaming, and once more he tried to seize hold of him with his telekinetic power. Rommel was barking nearby, each bark sounding like a cannon shot.

And at that moment, the Pacific Ocean reached up toward the priest.

He didn't see it coming, for his eyes at that moment were on Chuck. Even if he had seen it, it wouldn't have mattered. With a roar of a volcano, a wave thirty feet high rose up from the ocean that only moments before had been gently lapping at the edges of the pier. It crashed down upon the priest like a watery hand of God, drowning his screams in a rush of water. The priest flailed helplessly and Chuck could still make him out, a flickering image of black waving his hands frantically. And then the wave scooped the priest up and over the railing, to plunge into the Pacific.

Let him go! Rommel's advice sounded in his head. *He was boring anyway!*

Chuck not surprisingly, chose to ignore that advice. He leaped forward, using his TK power for an extra shove, and landed over by the railing, looking down frantically into the water to try to locate the priest.

The pier shook with greater anger, as if furious that Chuck was even trying to save the priest's life. Chuck went down to one knee and landed sharply on it, pain knifing through his leg. He grimaced, tried to reach out with his power, for he didn't necessarily need to see something to grab it up with his TK ability.

The crack of the wood beneath him was a moment too

late to warn him as a geyser of water exploded upward, hurling him into the air. It happened so quickly and with such concussive force that Chuck was momentarily stunned. Then he was sailing through the air, his arms pinwheeling madly, trying to find some sort of touchstone to lock on to.

For what seemed an infinity, he just appeared in his own mind to float, sailing like a graceful bird, the sounds of destruction and hysterics fading into the background and becoming a distant and faintly pleasant buzz.

Then he hit the water.

Greedily the ocean dragged him down and Chuck submerged.

The water stung his eyes, filled his lungs. It surged around him with unimaginable power and he felt himself in danger of being caught in some sort of undertow. His TK power was useless here. There was nothing to push off against, and he was too disoriented to do anything else except react with blind, if barely controlled, panic. He shucked off his heavy coat because it was dragging him down and started to kick furiously upward. His lungs were on fire, his limbs felt leaden, and somewhere inside him his brain was saying, *I'm not going to make it. I'm going to drown. I'm going to drown.*

And then another voice sounded in his head. A voice petulant and self-centered and angry, and it said, *If you drown, who's going to feed me?*

That certainly put things in perspective.

He kicked frantically, and hoped that his desperate thrusts were taking him in the right direction. He'd been turned around and flipped over so that he was totally disoriented. The water was surging around him and was so dark he couldn't even see his air bubbles to follow them to the surface.

The sound of his heart pounding was everywhere, and his brain was so oxygen-starved that, within seconds, it was going to force him to try to breathe.

He gave one final kick of his legs, propelled by desperation and more—by fury that all this had happened to him, that God had seen fit to dump all this on him and more and now he was going to wind up drowning. What a stupid, stupid way to . . .

He broke surface.

It was only for a moment and then he sank again, but seconds later his head surfaced for a second time. Greedily he gulped in air, gasping and spitting.

He looked around desperately. After all that, after feeling so remote, it turned out the pier was only a couple yards away. Then he saw something else . . . the priest, floating nearby. But the man was starting to slip under.

With powerful strokes, Chuck swam over to the priest and grabbed him under the arms just before the cleric could vanish again beneath the waves. Then he made his way back toward the pier and what could only laughingly be referred to as safety.

The rumbling had begun to subside, the waters also churning far less violently. The impromptu geysers that had been created in the wharf were mere trickles now. Yet Chuck could still hear the moans and sobbing, the frightened and frantic voices of people calling to each other, husbands shouting the names of wives, mothers crying out hysterically for their children.

Chuck made it to the edge of the pier and, using his TK power and no longer giving a damn who saw him, elevated the waterlogged priest onto the dock. He then hauled himself up and moments later was crouching next to the priest. Rommel hurried over, his concern for Chuck's safety carefully concealed within his usual attitude of I-don't-need-anybody.

The priest stared up at Chuck with lifeless eyes.

Chuck moaned softly and sat down next to the priest on the dock. Rommel poked at the unmoving cleric with his nose and turned to Chuck. *He's dead.*

"Yeah. Yeah, I know."

And for no reason that Chuck could determine, he was not afraid of further earthquake activity. It was as if the suddenly berserk activities of the earth and water had accomplished their purpose and was, therefore, no longer a threat. And their purpose was . . . what?

To kill the priest?

You can't be serious, said Rommel, in response to Chuck's unvoiced musing.

Was he serious? He wasn't sure. The priest had been talking nonsense, insanity. He had been claiming things that were part of fiction, not the everyday world.

Still . . .

If Jesus Christ had his second coming right now, right here, on modern twenty-first century earth . . . what would happen? Would he be believed? Would anyone know him for what he was? Would Chuck? Or would Chuck be one of the legions of people who would brush him off, laugh at him, eventually lock him away somewhere where he could go on with his rantings and not bother anybody.

He knew the answer. And he also knew that here was a man who had been terrified of something beyond the natural, and now he lay dead through mysterious means that had, at its most charitable, bizarre timing.

Rommel, looking around at the people who were staggering about the pier in shock, and the store owners who had just seen their livelihoods come down around their ears, said to Chuck, *This is the earthquake thing that humans were having fun at because it was pretend, right?*

"Right," said Chuck tiredly.

Some fun. I'm glad I'm a dog. At least my idea of fun doesn't kill people.

7

Matthew was eminently pleased with himself.

More than that, he felt almost giddy, as he made his way back to the respectable brownstone that was his home. It had become, at least for him, a lovely day, and so he was walking the several miles that he had cabbed earlier.

All around him, people were talking anxiously with each other about the earthquake that had localized around Pier 39. News trucks roared by, and everyone was walking around with a sort of tiptoe step to them, as if they were afraid that they might accidentally wake the ground up and make it rumble to infuriated life beneath them.

By contrast, Matthew was whistling, cheery. He would greet total strangers as he walked past them, and they looked at him oddly and even a little fearfully. With disaster so recent, it seemed almost sacrilegious to be upbeat and happy. One old woman, who Matthew smiled at with an enthusiastic, "Lovely day, isn't it?" even chided him about it.

"Lovely day?" she said. "You young fool! There are people dead!"

He shrugged and replied, "People die every day, lady," and then he went on his way, after making sure that a puddle in front of the woman turned to ice, causing her to slip and fall with a satisfying crack of bone. Her plaintive cries were music to him.

He stopped and bought a radio at an electronics store. He plugged the earphone into his ear and picked up a news station that was giving the latest statistics on the death and destruction caused by the totally unexpected, and unexplained, earthquake at Pier 39. There were nine people dead, twenty-seven injured, and property damage in the millions.

Of the property damage, Matthew did not care at all. As for the casualties, Matthew cared only about one—the priest.

He was definitely dead. Matthew had made sure that the priest had been under a good long time. He'd been certain that water had flooded the priest's lungs, giving him no way out and no hope. He had been very, very thorough. The other eight people dying were his responsibility too, of course. People who had taken fatal spills, or had had buildings collapse on them, or simply died of fright. But they were incidental. It had been the priest who was the target, and no one was going to pay attention to the death of one priest when an entire cataclysm had rocked their world.

No one was going to pay attention.

Except . . .

That guy. And his dog.

Matthew frowned over that. He didn't know who the priest was, but he had known that the priest was up to something. That perhaps the priest suspected—hell, knew—Matthew's abilities somehow. So he had disposed of the priest in an effective and untraceable way.

But what about the guy and the dog? They had shown

up when Matthew had fried Bill. Okay, fine. Happenstance. And then they'd shown up again at the hospital, but that could be ascribed to concern and conscientiousness.

Except these days, no one was concerned and conscientious. Everyone was out for themselves. That's simply the way things were.

But not this guy. This muscular guy, accompanied by a dog that looked like it could be saddled.

The first time, Matthew felt as if the dog had been looking for him specifically. That there was some sort of scent that the dog was tracking, but it was a scent beyond the olfactory. The dog was locked in on him, locked in on . . .

His mind? Could that be it? But that was insane. What, the dog was psychic? That was utterly ridiculous.

The man, though . . . he might be another story.

Matthew felt danger radiating from that man, and although Matthew was not afraid—he was far too powerful for that—he did feel concern nonetheless. Concern that somehow, this man was aware of him.

He had tried to dispatch the man and dog at the same time as he was disposing of the priest. But the man had fought back with far greater strength than Matthew would have anticipated. He had managed to outlast Matthew, for although he eventually had the man where he wanted him, Matthew was at that point too exhausted to carry on the attack any further. It was the most extended and most powerful stunt he had ever pulled, and he had been utterly drained by the time that mysterious man had floundered helplessly in the Pacific.

No matter. The priest was dead. Matthew had been too far away to hear what the priest was saying to the guy and his dog. Ultimately it was irrelevant. The priest wouldn't be around to say it any longer, and the man might just take this as a warning.

Yes. Matthew liked the sound of that. A warning to

mind his own business. To keep his nose clean. Destroying people, that was easy. But making them live in fear and terror of what could happen to them next—that sounded satisfyingly different.

He got to his home, and the moment he entered, a cry of joy was heard from within. He stopped, surprised and confused.

His mother was racing to him, embracing him desperately. She was a tall and aristocratic woman, with a polished diction that indicated her education and breeding. Her red hair fell in fashionable circlets around her face. At the moment she looked as if she were choking back tears.

"Oh, thank God, you're home, Matty!" she cried out. "Lyle! He's home! Matty's home!"

His face flushed and he muttered, "Mom, please . . . not Matty anymore, okay?"

His father came in from the other room, muttering into the headset phone that practically seemed glued to his head. "Yeah, he's back, I'll call you later," he was saying quickly, in that maddening way that always confused people as to whether he was conversing with them or with someone hundreds of miles away. He tapped the small red disconnect button situated just under the speaker and walked quickly across the parquet floor.

Where Carol Olivetti seemed to glide across a room, Lyle appeared to cut through it like a shark slicing through water on the way to a kill, leaving a large and sweeping wake behind him. He was half a head shorter than his wife, brown hair cut very short, his jaw jutting slightly forward in a bulldoggish manner that suggested he was always going straight for the jugular.

"Where the hell have you been?" demanded Lyle Olivetti. "Don't you know your mother's been worried sick about you?"

Matthew sighed. "No, I didn't know, because I thought

you guys weren't going to be home for a couple days yet."

Lyle hugged him in a perfunctory fashion. Matthew didn't much enjoy being embraced, and Lyle didn't like it either, so by silent mutual agreement they did it just enough to satisfy Carol's need to see some damned bonding or other. They broke contact after a moment.

His mother put an arm around him and steered him into the den. "We made sure to arrange our schedules so that we could be back early," she told him. "We wanted to surprise you. Then as soon as we got home we heard about this awful earthquake, and we didn't know where you were . . . well"—and she waved her hands about in vague, formless patterns—"we just got scared."

"Your mother was scared," said Lyle stiffly. "I had every confidence in you."

"Confidence is fine, Lyle, but there were eleven people killed," she told him sharply. "And you were nervous, don't pretend you weren't. You were the one on the phone with the police—"

"Eleven?" Matthew asked. "There were eleven people killed. I heard nine."

"Two more were found," she said with a touch of fear in her voice. Even though her son was clearly safe and sound at home, it wasn't enough to erase the chill from what was, to her, a close call. "Lyle, maybe we should just sell the house here and be done with it."

"I grew up in the Bay Area," said Lyle stiffly, "and if it was good enough for me, then it's good enough for my son."

"Mom, really, it's okay. See? I'm right here, I'm safe and sound. Besides, you know me. I always know how to take care of myself."

And he smiled pleasantly, and stopped worrying about the man and his dog.

Eleven bodies now. Maybe the man was among them. Who knew? Who cared?

As he allowed his mother to lead him into the kitchen, there to prepare a snack for him as she used to in the old days before maids and domestic help, Matthew's mind was racing.

He had encountered the man twice. Both times the man had come up short and, the second time, nearly dead. If it happened a third time—if they crossed swords once more—then Matthew would dispose of him. It was no more complicated than that.

He thought of something he'd read in a James Bond book—*Goldfinger*, he suspected. It was a short treatise on how to judge when someone is intentionally and deliberately going up against you, based on the number of times that they interfere with your plans. The line was, "Once is happenstance. Twice is coincidence. Three times is enemy actions."

If the man and dog came up against him a third time, it would be definite enemy action. And Matthew would make certain that they went the way of the priest.

8

I really hate this, Rommel informed him.

Chuck finished placing the leash and muzzle over Rommel's head. "Stop complaining. You want to stay somewhere decent, don't you? Besides, in any case the Complex is looking for us—and when aren't they—this will be a helpful disguise."

I really hate this, Rommel informed him in no uncertain terms, unimpressed by Chuck's pleadings.

Chuck had purchased a small suitcase that was sitting next to the open door of the RAC 3000. The car was commenting tartly, "Muzzles and leashes on wild animals are always to be preferred."

"He's not a wild animal, Rac, and it's just for convenience sake."

Rac made no reply, but Rommel growled ominously and wondered whether chewing on the tires would blow one of them out. As it happened, all it would have done was break Rommel's teeth, what with the new puncture-proof tires. Rommel didn't know that and, by happy circumstance, didn't have occasion to find out.

Chuck removed the darkened glasses from his jacket pocket and gripped the leash. "Okay, Rac. Lock down."

The door swung shut and all of Rac's alarm systems immediately snapped on. The parking garage was a block away from the hotel. It wouldn't have done for Chuck to go driving up to the hotel garage, especially considering what he was about to do.

With his free hand he picked up the suitcase and, holding the leash firmly, said, "Let's go."

The desk clerk at the San Francisco Executive Hotel did not like surprises. He also did not like dogs. So when a dog showed up as a surprise, it certainly wasn't going to thrill him a bit.

"Excuse me!" he said sharply to the man walking the monstrous German shepherd through the tastefully decorated lobby of the hotel. "Excuse me, you can't bring that animal in here!"

The man who was walking the dog looked around quizzically . . .

No. Didn't look around. The desk clerk gulped as he realized his error. The man walking the dog was blind. He wore sunglasses, and had the air of someone who was trying to listen to everything from all directions. His head moved about like a conning tower, absorbing everything.

"Sir," said the clerk in a decidedly less belligerent voice. "Over here, sir. Straight ahead."

The man nodded gratefully and, gripping his small suitcase with clear nervousness, allowed the dog to lead him to the front desk. Patrons who were seated in the lobby, even if they were nowhere near the man's path, got out of his way nevertheless. Part of it was deference to the handicapped, and part of it was pure fear of the huge canine that was his guide.

The moment the man was close enough, the clerk said in a lowered voice, "I'm terribly sorry about before, sir."

"Aren't seeing-eye dogs permitted?" the man asked. Despite his muscular build, he seemed shy, even tentative. Well, it was to be expected.

"Oh, of course they are," the clerk hurried to assure him. "It's just that they're usually much"—he looked at the dog, who appeared to be glaring back at him—"much more sedate."

"Oh, Rommel's big, I know," said the man affectionately, patting the dog on the head. The dog didn't seem to especially like being petted, but did nothing to force the man to stop . . .

(Like what? Eat him?)

"It's just that," continued the man, "the way things are nowadays, in some of the cities . . . you know how it is."

"I understand fully, sir," said the desk clerk. "Such an animal must provide quite a feeling of security."

"Oh, yes." The man smiled. "Yes indeed."

Several minutes later Chuck and Rommel were upstairs, ensconced in a fairly decent room courtesy of one of the bogus Cards that Wyatt Wonder had provided him.

Rommel wandered around, poking and prodding at such strange objects as the shoe buffer. Chuck, for his part, had dumped his few belongings into one of the dresser drawers and tossed his sunglasses onto a nearby bed. Rommel had made very loud and decisive noises until Chuck removed the muzzle from him, and even though the sham had gotten them a nice room at a nice place, Rommel still made it clear that such amenities were secondary in importance to being able to move his mouth freely.

To quiet Rommel, Chuck ordered up room service, requesting and getting two raw steaks for Rommel, and a burger and fries for himself. While they waited for the food to come up, Chuck rummaged through the three local newspapers that he'd purchased and hidden in his suitcase. (Somehow it would seem to blow his cover if a blind man walked in with newspapers under his arm.)

He scanned every one of them from beginning to end. He read write-up after write-up about the destruction of the previous day, including multiple attempts by respected scientists to explain the unexplainable. Naturally there was no mention of himself, or pictures, for he had made sure to be nowhere near by the time the press and authorities were showing up.

He did see one picture in the *Herald* in which he could clearly make out the unmoving form of the priest on the pier. He hadn't wanted to just abandon him there, but there really hadn't been much choice. Toting around the body of a priest seemed rather pointless, and not exactly low profile.

Chuck heard some sort of distant murmurings from the street below and glanced out. His eyes widened as, once again, he saw snow falling. This time it was coming down even harder than before. Hapless pedestrians were scattering, unsure of what to make of this. People would point upward nervously and chatter at each other, and Chuck really couldn't blame them. Californians were adaptable to such expected disasters as earthquakes, but snow? A white Christmas? Absurd.

There was no Carmen Friedman listed in the phone book or newspapers.

He started calling them up, and at the first newspaper he simply got an operator saying that no such person was there. The second newspaper however, the *Tribune*, got a brisk, "I'll connect you."

He held on, holding his breath and not sure why.

A brisk female voice came on the other end. "Carmen Friedman . . ."

"Ms. Friedman. I'm—" he began.

But the voice continued at a staccato pace, ". . . isn't here right now. Leave a message and she'll get back to you."

A beep sounded that was a tad too loud, bordering on earsplitting. Chuck winced against it.

"Ms. Friedman," he said carefully, "a mutual, pious friend said that you would be a good person to talk to about a certain young man. The friend is now with the Heavenly Father. I'm at the Executive Hotel, Room 420, if you'd like to talk. I'll be waiting here for your call."

He hung up and sat back, steepling his fingers and thinking.

He was surrounded by flames.

Chuck staggered about, screaming, his feet sinking into what appeared to be molten lava. All around him was the overpowering stench of burning human flesh and brimstone. An ungodly stink that caused him to wretch deeply. He pulled his feet upward, as if wading through a huge, burning swamp, and he screamed Rommel's name. There was no answer. He screamed out to God on high, and still there was no answer.

Grips apparently carved right from rock stuck out at odd angles from the wall nearby. He lunged toward them and howled as the heat of the wall threatened to sear the skin right from hid fingers. Gritting his teeth, he pulled himself upward, extracting his tortured feet one at a time from the scalding mire. The pain was overwhelming to the point where he was beyond pain. His brain had shut down the pain centers, unable to cope with what he was facing.

He pulled himself up, looking in horror at the burning and ruined mass that had been his feet. He sobbed, calling the name of his ex-wife, Anna. The pain and heat from the wall were still intense, but it was secondary compared to what was roiling in front of him.

The air was thick with red haze and there were the screams and moans of the damned from all around him. He added his own voice to it, crying out for help, for aid, for something.

The hideous mess that was his feet sought purchase on the narrow rocky ledge above the boiling miasma. He glanced around desperately, trying to find some way out.

And then the boiling pool in front of him began to bubble and swirl, like a whirlpool. He looked at it in confusion and fear. His clothes were hanging in tatters, his skin reddened and becoming black.

A figure began to emerge from the pool. It rose straight up, imposing and terrifying, and Chuck whimpered as he faced it.

It was a kid. A teenager. With horns, and a narrow, evil face, and eyes glowing yellow, like a snake's eyes. His mouth drew back in a bemused smile, exposing dripping fangs. He was naked but his skin was beet red and glowing with unearthly power.

Chuck's mouth moved but no sound came out.

"Hello," said the entity. "I understand you've been looking for me." Then he laughed, a high-pitched laugh like bats squeaking, like nails across a chalkboard, and he reached for Chuck. Chuck only had time for one high-pitched, horrified scream, and then he was dragged down off his perch. He was pulled under the flowing lava, felt it fill his mouth and ooze down into his lungs and stomach, and everywhere was fire.

And a sound, a loud, overpowering deafening sound, like bombs dropping, that drowned out everything, even the frantic pumping of his heart.

Barking . . .

Chuck sat up, gasping, sweat pouring down him. His T-shirt was pasted to his chest.

Rommel's forepaws were up on the bed and he was barking at Chuck, each bark so loud it seemed to shake the furniture. There was an angry pounding from overhead as whoever was in the room above Chuck's made clear his displeasure over being awakened at . . .

Chuck cast his bleary eyes at the clock. Two in the morning.

What was your problem? demanded Rommel.

Chuck moaned and slowly sank back onto the pillow. The sheet beneath him was also sopping from the perspiration, and it was then that Chuck realized he'd forgotten to put on the air-conditioning. "Bad dream," muttered Chuck. "I was . . . I was in hell."

What's hell?

Chuck was rubbing his chest, feeling a sharp pain caused by the pounding of his heart. He stepped out of bed to go over to the air-conditioner.

What's hell? Rommel asked again. *Is it very hot?*

"Yes," Chuck said. "How did you know?"

I sensed it. In your mind.

"Hell is where Satan lives," said Chuck, and then after a moment added, ". . . or his son."

Who's Satan?

Chuck glanced at Rommel, amused. "Satan is responsible for all the evil in the world."

Oh, said Rommel. *I thought humans were.*

"Well . . . we are, I guess."

So Satan must be human, and the world must be hell.

Chuck stared at Rommel. "For a dog who, a couple of months ago, couldn't grasp the concept of measurement, you're getting pretty damned sharp. I can see I'm not going to be getting back to sleep tonight."

And as if to underscore that, the phone rang.

Chuck stared at it in surprise, and then picked it up. "Yeah?"

A female voice—the same that had been speaking on the answering machine before—said, "This is Carmen Friedman. You called me?"

"You work strange hours, Ms. Friedman," he said.

"Goes with the job. You knew Father Pertwee."

"In passing." He took a breath and plunged in. "He told me something really incredible, about—"

"No," she said quickly. "Not now. We won't discuss this now. Come to the newspaper, tomorrow. Twelve noon. Don't tell anyone you're coming here."

"All right," said Chuck, feeling very clandestine. "Not that I was planning to. But why all the caution?"

"Because," she said, "we don't want word to get out. If people knew what was going on, all hell could break loose." She hung up on him before he could say another word.

He stared at the telephone.

"There's a cheerful analogy," he muttered.

9

Chuck stood in front of the *Tribune* building, craning his neck and looking upward. It was tall and imperious, and evoked in Chuck a memory of a time that, in fact, he did not recall. A time when there was something called a First Amendment. One of the things it said was that people could talk about whatever they wanted, and write about whatever they wanted, without interference from the government.

This had, of course, gone the way of the dodo.

Chuck, with Rommel at his side, walked into the lobby and consulted with a woman at an information desk, who called up to the city room and got the clearance needed from someone—presumably, Carmen—for him to come up. But when Chuck and Rommel tried to proceed, immediately a guard stopped them. He pointed sternly at Rommel and said, "No dogs allowed upstairs."

Chuck looked down at Rommel, and then back up at the guard. "You sure?"

"Positive," said the guard. "Building rules."

Chuck shrugged. He wasn't especially worried about Rommel's ability to take care of himself. "Fine. Rommel, wait here." And he headed for the elevator.

"Wait a minute! You can't leave him here!"

Chuck didn't even glance back. "Oh, he'll be fine."

The guard looked at Rommel and gulped. Rommel stared at him impassively.

"He's supposed to have a leash!" the guard shouted.

Chuck turned and, reaching into his pocket, pulled out a worn leash. He tossed it to Rommel, who caught it in his teeth. "Gotta obey the law, Rommel."

He stepped into the elevator, leaving the guard sputtering. The guard looked at Rommel, who was sitting there benignly with the leash in his huge jaws.

The guard gulped.

Chuck stepped off the elevator that opened directly into the city room.

It was quiet.

Deathly quiet.

He frowned. His image of what city rooms were like was largely shaped from old films he had seen. People shouting "Rewrite!" and "Copy boy!" and "Stop the presses!" All of it surrounded with a pounding urgency to get the story out, to meet the deadlines, to inform the people and try to accomplish some good.

Now, of course, many of the old sounds of newsrooms were gone. There were no clattering of teletypes or pounding of typewriter keyboards. These noisy implements had been replaced by streamlined computers and laser printers. But it was more than the electronic materials that had been eliminated. There was an ambience that was gone. Instead . . . there were walls.

City rooms had usually been large affairs where all the desks were visible, where people shouted to each other. But now there were dozens of partitions, multicolored and covered with some sort of felt material. Nobody could see anybody.

There were a series of offices along the wall—the city editor, the national editor, and so on. And one more thing. Positioned in front of the offices was a long, horseshoe-shaped desk. Three men were seated around it, and there was room for a fourth, but the chair was empty. Each of the three men, who looked like they'd been stamped from cookie cutters, were in front of computer monitors and were studying the words flashing by. On occasion their fingers would fly over the keyboards, making some sort of adjustment. Their expressions never changed.

"Can I help you?"

Chuck turned and there was a man in a gray suit, who looked very similar to the other men in the other gray suits who were seated a short distance away around the horseshoe table. His lips were as thin as his hair.

"I'm looking for Carm—"

"You shits!"

Chuck glanced around in confusion. A female voice had just shouted an outraged profanity, and he was more than a little curious to know what had prompted it.

A woman came storming out from within the maze of partitions. Her obvious fury startled several reporters into peering out, groundhoglike, from their partitions.

She was not a tall woman. She had short-cropped brown hair, a round face, and walked aggressively with her shoulders thrust forward. She was wearing a loud Hawaiian shirt that was not tucked in to her tight jeans. She sported large glasses that obscured most of her face, but it was still obvious that her expression was one of seething fury.

The men at the horseshoe desk looked up in unison, their expressions still unchanging.

"Which one of you shits did it?" she demanded, thumping her fist on the desk. "Come on! Which one of you killed my story?"

The gray man sighed softly and walked away from Chuck, heading over to the woman. "A problem, Miss Friedman?" he asked calmly.

She turned on him. "Which one of your bozos killed my story, Erwin? Which one?"

The man she had addressed as Erwin stared down at her, his lips becoming (if possible) even thinner than before. "That story being the alleged charges brought against the dean of U.C.L.A.?"

"You know damned well that's the story I'm talking about."

He raised a scolding finger. "Language, Miss Friedman, please. As for your story—the charges aren't proven yet."

She clenched her fists and waved them in the air. "Of course they haven't been proven. That's what the article is about! *Alleged* wrongdoing. The evidence I've got in there is incontrovertible."

"There's no need to upset matters when nothing has been proven," said Erwin. "If the dean had been tried and convicted, that would be one thing. You make all sorts of charges that haven't even been studied by a grand jury yet."

Her teeth clenched, and she looked ready to hit him. Chuck now saw the city editor emerging from his office.

"It is not our place," Erwin said, "to make the news, but only report the news. Your investigations are laudable, but unless formal charges have been made and proven—"

"It's articles like this one that get those charges made!" snapped Friedman.

"The government appreciates your help," said Erwin, "but the government is more than capable of launching its own investigations, wherever and whenever they are deemed necessary." Making it clear that that, as far as he was concerned, was the last word, Erwin went to his chair and sat down.

The city editor stepped in quickly as Carmen Friedman took a step toward Erwin, who wasn't even doing her the

honor of looking her way. Instead he was already con-
centrating on a computer screen, clearly having put the
conversation behind him and gone on to the next matter.
The city editor kept an arm around Carmen and led her
away, speaking to her in a steady, determined, and low
voice. The show over, the other reporters retreated to the
relative safety of their cubbies.

Chuck, utterly confused, stared after them. As he
passed by the horseshoe desk, he was suddenly addressed
by Erwin who said quietly, "Are you a friend of Miss
Friedman's?"

"We, uhm . . . we haven't officially met, yet."

"Yes, well, Mr. . . . ?"

Chuck suddenly felt very uncomfortable under Erwin's
gaze. "Green," he said. "Chuck Green."

Erwin sat back, staring at him, regarding him with curiosity. "May I ask what you want with Miss Friedman?"
He pulled a couple of small bottles of water from under
his desk and offered one to Chuck.

"I'm not really thirsty," said Chuck.

Erwin actually smiled, which was mildly chilling. "Really. I insist. Best water in California. That's because it
comes from upstate New York."

Chuck shrugged and took the bottle, twisting off the
top and taking a swig.

"So . . . Miss Friedman?" prompted Erwin.

"Oh . . . it's nothing, really," said Chuck.

"Is it regarding a story?"

"A story? Oh. No, no, not a story." Chuck shook his
head, adopting his best "aw-shucks" manner. "I really
don't know much about newspapers or stories or such.
No, it's a personal matter, actually."

"And it would be—?" Erwin prompted.

Chuck smiled evenly. "Personal," he said with finality.
He finished the water and admitted to himself that it had
tasted pretty good. Too bad the bottle had been so small.
He put it back on the desk and walked off in the direction

that he had seen Friedman go. Erwin watched him with narrow eyes.

Chuck spent a few minutes peering around corners into cubbies, apologizing to reporters whom he disturbed. It was odd, though. He would have thought that reporters would have an aggressive, hard-bitten attitude. But these men and women—they seemed bitter, even defeated. It was very, very strange.

Finally he found the one he was looking for. In it, Carmen Friedman was sitting, fuming, drumming her fingers on the desktop. He watched her pull open a drawer and take out a packet of cigarettes. She sat there and stared at them.

"Need a light?" asked Chuck. He didn't know why he was asking. He didn't smoke, and didn't have a match or a lighter on him.

"No," she sighed. "No, I quit six months ago. Just, every so often, I take them out and stare at them. Makes me feel better. Fondle them a little. Makes me feel like a woman."

"Oh. Well . . . it's better that you quit. Healthier. There's enough things in the air these days as it is. No need to pollute your lungs further."

She turned and stared at him, peering over the top of her glasses. "Can I help you with something? Or do you want to stand there all day discussing my bronchial tubes?"

"Oh. I'm sorry. Uhm . . . we had an appointment?"

Her eyes seemed to snap into focus on him. "Yeah. Room 420, right?"

"Right."

She sat back and stared at him, sizing him up. "So you knew Pertwee, huh?"

"In a manner of speaking."

She waved him to the only other chair in the cramped cubicle. As he sat, he chucked a thumb in the general direction of the horseshoe desk. "What was all that about?"

"That," she said sourly, "is the government editors' table."

"What's that?"

"All stories," she said, "go through that desk, to be checked for what they call 'accuracy.' It's nothing but a censorship board. What they say goes, including whatever stories they don't like."

"Like the story about the dean."

"Uh-huh. Now, of course, the fact that the dean was a major contributor to the president's last campaign—well, that wouldn't have anything to do with it, now, would it."

"Do all newspapers have them?"

"The major ones, like us, have them on premises. Smaller newspapers sometimes wind up sharing a single local government editorial office. Thanks to the computer world we live in, stories can all be modemed instantaneously for inspection and approval. But all articles go through them."

He shook his head. "I never heard of them."

"Of course you haven't. Where would you have heard of them?"

"Well, I suppose I . . ." He stopped, realizing. And knowing that he knew, she nodded.

"Right. You would have read about them in the papers, or seen something in the news. But you didn't. Of course you didn't. You think they're going to allow stories about themselves to circulate?" She made a rude noise.

"That's—that's terrible," he said. "Something should be done."

"Absolutely," she said. "Let's run a story about it. Get people stirred up."

"Oh," he said softly.

"Yeah. Oh. So—what did Pertwee tell you?"

He stroked his chin for a moment. The concentration from the woman upon him was almost palpable. Chuck took a breath. "Pertwee told me about someone who he said is Satan's son."

"Matthew Olivetti," she said immediately.

He was startled. "So Pertwee really did come and talk to you."

"Oh, yeah. And I've done some digging. Found out some weird stuff. But what's your interest in it?"

"Pertwee felt that I should know."

"Yeah?" She leaned forward and spoke quickly, sharply. "Listen to me. The stuff that I'm involved with, you want to steer clear of. There are some seriously rotten things going on with Olivetti. We're talking dead people. We're talking maimed people. We're talking stuff you don't even want to know about. I think Olivetti is a powerful player—maybe more powerful than anybody can guess. And you know what else? I'll never be able to get it past the watchdogs up there. So the last thing I need is some amateur wandering in and sticking his nose into the middle of it. I don't know who you are, or what your interest is. My guess is that you're another writer who's trying to horn in on my story. Forget it, buster. It's mine. I don't know if I'll ever be able to do anything with it, but it's mine. So why don't you just move off, okay?"

He stared at her. "You brought me all the way here to tell me that?"

"Yeah. When I tell people to blow off, I like to look 'em in the eye."

He nodded slowly.

Then he took her cigarette pack away, without touching it. One moment the pack was in her hand, the next it was floating in front of her. She gulped and stared at it. It dangled in front of Chuck's unsmiling face.

"Crunch," he said.

The pack of cigarettes promptly crunched up with a crackling of cellophane.

He allowed them to drop back to the desk. She regarded them for a long moment, and then looked back at him. It was clear that a question was poised on her lips, but she didn't ask it. Instead she said, "You a cousin of his?"

"Of—whose? Olivetti's?"

She nodded.

"No. Not by blood, at any rate. Can he do that?"

"What, crumple cigarette packs? I'm not sure. But I'll tell you, there's not a hell of a lot he can't do."

She turned to her computer and punched in some key words. A file flashed on her screen and she studied it carefully.

"If that's the best you can do," she said, without looking at him, "Matthew Olivetti will take you apart."

"I wouldn't bet on that."

"I would." She clicked off her computer and stood. "Come on. Not here. The walls have ears."

"Really. Wish I had the Q-tip concession."

They walked through the city room and past the horseshoe table. Carmen paused a moment to stick her tongue out at Erwin, who disdained to look at her. She walked out with Chuck in tow.

But as they went out, Erwin looked up and watched them. Then he reached down into his desk drawer and pulled out the now-empty bottle of water that Chuck had been drinking earlier. It was neatly sealed in a plastic bag.

"Ned," he said to the man sitting next to him, "have this sent to the lab for analysis. Run a check on any prints aside from my own."

Ned took the bag and stared at the contents. "What are you expecting to find?"

"I don't know," said Erwin. "Just a hunch about the man who was handling it. And I've learned to trust my hunches."

10

Carmen was seated in the passenger seat of Rac, looking around nervously. The thing she was most determined not to look at was the massive dog in the back seat. "What's his name again?" she asked.

"Rommel."

"And how many people has he eaten recently?"

"None. Not recently."

"Ohhhh, good," she said. "And the car knows the way, you said."

Chuck was sitting with his hands disconcertingly laced behind his head. The car was moving without his guidance. "You said you wanted to go to Golden Gate Academy. Rac's got the address down in her records, don't you, Rac?"

"Golden Gate Academy is listed in the local directory, Charles," Rac informed him.

Carmen shook her head. "You must have some serious bucks behind you to be in a car like this. I've heard of these things, but never ridden in one."

"Oh, they're great," he told her.

"Can you put some music on?"

"Sure. What do you want to hear?"

"How about something from Salt and Pepper?"

"Ah," said Chuck, smiling. "So you're into old rock stars trying to make a comeback, huh?"

"Hey, look," she said. "I remember Madonna and Michael Jackson when they were young and could really belt out a number. So now they're older, want to team up as Salt and Pepper to try to revive the old times . . . that's just ginger peachy with me."

"Whatever you say. Rac—Salt and Pepper, please. Maybe their latest album, 'Please Abuse Me.' "

Deep orchestral notes filled the car. Carmen frowned. "What the hell is that?"

"Beethoven," Rac informed her.

"Beethoven?" Carmen said incredulously. "The old deaf kraut? That guy? I thought we were getting Michael and Madonna."

"No," said Chuck, holding up a finger. "We *asked* for Michael and Madonna. With Rac, what you ask for and what you get aren't always the same."

"Well, that sucks. And you knew that? Then why did you let me ask?"

"Because misery loves company," he replied. "So why are we going to Golden Gate?"

"I'll answer one if you answer one."

"Shoot."

"Okay. Who the hell are you?"

He sighed softly. "You really want to know?"

"Oh, heck no. I'm only a reporter. I don't *really* want to find out things. I just want to spend the day jerking around and collecting my paycheck."

"I'll take that as a yes." He paused. "My name is Chuck Simon."

"Jesus Christ."

He stroked the beard. "You think we look that much alike?"

"I thought you could be Simon," she said, "when you pulled the levitation bit. These days, there's more guys running around with TK powers than you would think. But it was too much to hope for. Chuck Simon. The guy at the head of the government's 'gee-we'd-like-to-nail-this-bastard' list."

"You've obviously heard of me."

"Heard of you? I cracked your damned story."

He nodded. "And the Rover boys wouldn't let you print it."

"That's right. Quashed because of national security."

She shook her head. "I remember when being a reporter meant going after the government, not being sat on by it. But I digress . . ." She regarded Chuck with an upraised eyebrow. "Yeah. Yeah, I was pretty sure it was you. Guy with TK power. Government wants him to be an assassin, and he hightails it out with a coconspirator."

"A coconspirator?" said Chuck. "Now that's news."

"News is my business."

"What coconspirator?"

"My sources were fuzzy on that. All they said was that it was some guy with a German name."

Chuck tried not to laugh at that, and failed. "German name? You mean like Beethoven?"

She smiled thinly. "Not quite."

"How about Rommel?" He indicated the dog with a nod of his head.

She stared at him. "Ohhh, my God. You're kidding."

"Guess the sources leave something to be desired, huh?"

She frowned. "I'll kill him."

"Who?"

"My government source. He said all he knew was the guy had a German name, and was a real animal. He decided to have his private joke with me. Ha ha ha. See how amused I am. I'm so amused I'm going to kill the creep when I see him again."

"So I answered your question," Chuck reminded her. "Now you answer mine. Why did you get involved with all this?"

She sighed. "Pertwee married me."

He looked at her incredulously. "You were married to a priest?"

"No, you fathead," she said. "He performed the marriage. I got married in my twenties, to a guy who wasn't Jewish—which just thrilled my parents, I can tell you. Pertwee performed the wedding ceremony. The marriage split after a couple years, but I would still hear from Pertwee every so often. Then one day he waltzes into the newspaper, sputtering and stuttering about this kid he's fixated on. You know me. Reporter instinct goes off."

"You thought the kid was dangerous?"

"Nah," said Friedman. She pulled a stick of gum from her jacket pocket and pulled off the wrapper. "I figured Pertwee was gay. He'd fallen in love with the kid, and didn't know how to deal with it. So I started doing some digging, figuring I'd find out some interesting stuff. Even our beloved government watchdogs would let a story like that go through—a priest acting corrupt with a teenager. Our beloved government is homophobic, after all. Just like all governments."

"You mean," said Chuck incredulously, "that you were willing to publicize what you believed to be a homosexual affair, just for the purpose of writing a story that would see print?"

"Of course. I'm a reporter. A damned good one." She tossed the gum in her mouth and started chewing.

"I'm shocked."

"Try being a reporter for a while," she said. "You'll find your shocker gets pretty worn down. At any rate, your wounded sense of propriety can go back into its case. You see, I didn't find anything like that. I didn't find anything I expected to find. What I found, frankly, scares the living crap out of me. And that takes some doing, because if there's one thing I'm filled with, it's living crap. Turn here," she said, forgetting for a moment that Chuck wasn't driving.

"I was already turning, Miss Friedman," Rac informed her briskly as the car turned sharply and pulled up in front of the school.

Chuck and Carmen stepped out of the car and Rommel eased his massive body out from the back. Chuck looked at the main entrance of the unassuming building. "What are we doing here?" he asked.

She gestured for him to follow and she walked to the front door. She pulled on it and it was locked. "Now what?" he asked.

"Do your stuff," she said.

He looked taken aback. "My stuff?"

"I know your background. I know what you can do. Now get us in here."

"That's breaking and entering!"

"There's something I have to check out."

"Can't we check it out out here?" he asked.

"No. Now come on. I haven't got all day."

What's the problem?

"She wants me to break into this school," Chuck informed Rommel.

Friedman looked from man to dog. "You talking to him?"

"Of course."

"Of course," she shrugged. "Coconspirators should always stay in touch."

So break in.

"It's wrong."

Does it have to do with whatever caused that kid to burn?

Chuck paused. "Yes. Yes, I think it does."

And to Chuck's amazement, Rommel sounded deadly serious. *Do whatever you have to. Please.*

The plea from his dog was nothing short of astounding to Chuck. "Okay, okay. I'll do it."

Thanks.

Chuck reached out with his mind and into the locking mechanism. He felt the various tumblers and deadbolts in it. More modern systems might have had some sort of computer locks, which would have been much harder for him to deal with. But this was definitely not a modern system.

He sweated for a few long moments, fine-tuning his concentration, and then was rewarded with the loud sounds of locks unclicking. Carmen nodded, impressed, and pushed in on the door. It swung open without protest. "Not bad," she said.

Chuck wiped away the sweat from his brow and looked up. Snow was beginning to fall gently again. "Weird," he said.

"That might be the work of our young friend," she said, and gestured for him to follow. He did so, Rommel right behind him.

They walked through the school hallway, the only noise to be heard coming from the click of Rommel's nails on the tile floor. Carmen was glancing around, checking the labels on the doors, and Chuck tried to fight down nervousness. What in God's name did he have to be nervous about, after all? They were going to encounter some old janitor or something? Perhaps—unlikely as it seemed—a security guard? Chuck had dispatched assassins, trained killers, soldiers. There was absolutely no reason for him to worry about whatever the school might throw at him.

The school had an austere, old-world feeling about it. Clearly there was great pride in tradition there. The walls were lined with various trophies that had been awarded in various competitions. Athletic, academic—the school had it all.

Including just possibly, a homicidal lunatic.

"Here," she said, stopping in front of a door that was labeled "Office." She worked the knob. Locked. She gestured to Chuck, who barely had to give this one a moment's thought. The door sprung open.

"Will you marry me?" she asked.

"Never on a first date."

They slid in and she looked around. It looked to Chuck like any other school office he had ever seen. He had been a teacher once, in a life that seemed as if it had been an existence of another man entirely.

She went straight to the file cabinets, her fingers skimming along the clearly labeled drawers, before she found the one she wanted. She wanted. She pulled the drawer open and started rummaging.

"Remember," she was saying as she did so, "remember how when you were in school, and if you did something—no matter how trivial—the teacher would always warn you, 'That's going to go into your permanent file'?"

"Uh-huh."

"Well, that's what we've got here," she said triumphantly, pulling out a thick manila folder from the drawer. She turned and laid it down on a desk. "The permanent file of one Matthew Olivetti."

"Have you seen this before?"

"Nope. Everything I've found on him, I've turned up on computer records, old newspaper clippings, that sort of thing. But this . . ."

Her voice trailed off as she placed the folder down on the desk and began to study it. Chuck looked over her shoulder. She was examining report cards, correspondence—years' worth of material in his folder.

Then she reached into her jacket pocket and pulled out a steno notebook. She flipped it open and laid it down next to the file folder. There was a list of names in it, and she glanced back and forth, making notations and jotting them down.

"Find anything interesting?" he asked.

"Well, that depends how you define 'interesting.' Take this, for example." She pulled out one report card and flipped to the comments on the back. "This is from third grade. A Mrs. Potts, his teacher, writes, 'Matthew is very sullen and uncooperative. He should be doing more to socialize with other children.' And see, she gave him an 'Unsatisfactory' in classroom behavior. It was the only black mark on his report card. But the next quarter's comments are by a Miss Briggs, and she simply writes, 'Matthew is very quiet, but some children are that way. He could try to be friendlier, but I'm sure he'll come around.' "

"What happened to Mrs. Potts?" asked Chuck.

She glanced back at her notebook to confirm what she already knew. "Mrs. Potts," she said quietly, "was pregnant . . . and died in childbirth."

"Died?"

"Yeah. Died. And here's a bit of timing. It happened the day after the report card with her comments came out."

"It could still be coincidence."

"According to my research, she wasn't due for three months. Up until that time, it was a normal pregnancy. Then one day, while she was in class, there was suddenly a totally unexpected, inexplicable earthquake. And she, lucky devil, was at the epicenter. She lost the baby and died right afterward of shock. And guess who was in her class at the time."

"That's not conclusive," said Chuck uncertainly.

"Now here's something interesting," said Carmen, as if she hadn't even heard him. "A letter from Matthew's parents, when he was in fifth grade. They're complaining about a school bully, one Darryl Schweitzer. Said Darryl was picking on their precious boy. Said the school should stop it. Guess what?" She looked at her own notebook.

"According to my notes, one Darryl Schweitzer was up high on the monkey bars during recess and fell off. Kids said a totally bizarre gust of wind knocked him off on what had been a perfectly calm day. Broke his arm and leg—missed the rest of the school year. Compared to Mrs. Potts, he got off lucky."

Chuck pulled over a wheeled chair and sat next to her. "How much more have you got?"

"I checked school records," she said, "of each class that little Matthew was in, all the way to now, his senior year. Then I ran checks on their names for any sort of unusual accidents. Now, of course, things happen to people, or to people they know, as they grow up. It's part of life. When I was a kid, I had a friend who got hit by a truck and landed, wedged, under a parked car. I remember standing there, watching them have to get the parked car off him with a crane or something. Like I said, it happens. What's interesting is that it happens with consistency among little Matthew's peers. Matt moved around a few times. His parents are well-to-do. Extremely so, in fact. So Matt has been educated in New York and London, as well as being the pride of the Bay Area. That's part of the reason that the accidents haven't gotten noticed. They've been spread out."

"Even if they did notice them," said Chuck slowly. "No one would make the connection with him."

"Nope," agreed Carmen. "No reason to. Look here . . ."

Over the next few minutes she was able to find half a dozen examples of people who had criticized or somehow crossed swords with Matthew Olivetti, and had lived to regret it . . . or had not lived at all.

Chuck sat back, letting out a long *pheewwwww* sound. Then he shook his head. "I still find it hard to believe—impossible, really—that he's some sort of Satan spawn." Then his eyes narrowed. "He's not. He's like me. He's a psionic. And he's consistent."

She frowned. "What do you mean, 'consistent'?"

"Look. Everything that's happened in connection with him—it's of some sort of elemental nature. The four elements of ancient belief. Earth, air, water, and fire."

"Wasn't that an old musical group?"

"I'm serious," he said. "Look. Earthquakes. Gust of wind. Drownings. Incinerations. All of them, extending from that basic concept."

"So what are you saying?"

"I'm . . ." he paused. "I don't know what I'm saying. I don't know what I'm talking about—except that he's psionic, like me. I'd bet my life on it."

He sat there for a moment, considering it. "Think about this. He obviously learned, early on, of his abilities. He's known for years what he can do. The whole concept of growing up is in learning about what you can and can't do. Learning the parameters. Living within them. But here comes this kid, and he comes to realization that the rules for him are different than they are for other people."

"No they're not," said Carmen firmly.

"Yes they are," replied Chuck. "Oh, yes they are. When you can do something that other people can't—when you can control the earth beneath your feet, or the sky overhead . . ." His voice trailed off. "My God, the sky. The snow. You think he's causing the snow?"

"I—I don't know," she said in a small voice, sounding surprisingly meek.

"It's possible. Anything's possible, with him. That's what I was saying. You learn of the infinite possibilities, and at that age, you can't deal with it. I can barely deal with it at my age. And that does something to you. It has to. When you can manipulate the real world, the way that he did. If the real world has no rules for you, how can you put together rules for yourself?"

"So what are you saying? That it's all right for him to murder and kill and do whatever he wants?"

"No! No, I'm not saying that at all. What I'm saying

is that when you're in first and second and third grade, you pull the wings off flies because it seems like it would be an interesting thing to do. You want to see what will happen when you do it. But there are limits as to what you can do in your childish quest to see 'what will happen.' But if you're capable of doing the things this kid can do, then there are no limits. The sky that he controls is the limit.

"So he learns that at a young age. He learns he can do whatever the hell he wants. And he learns to control it, to conceal it, like a secret because he's afraid that somehow someone's going to take it away from him. But no one does, and no one discovers that he's doing these things. And time passes and he becomes more and more confident and sure of himself. Until . . ."

"Until he becomes a teenager," she said. "And decides that he can rule the world."

"Which he just might be able to do," agreed Chuck.

They looked at each other.

"Time to go visit with the heir apparent of the world," said Carmen Friedman.

11

Matthew Olivetti was lying back on his bed, his hands tucked behind his head, when his mother bustled in in that way she had that indicated to Matthew that he was going to have a problem.

"Yeah, Mom?" he said without enthusiasm.

"We're having visitors tomorrow," she told him happily.

He made no reply. There didn't seem to be much point. Whether there were visitors or not seemed of little interest to him.

"People are coming over from the newspaper. They want to interview myself and your father."

"So?" This was not exactly a hot news item. People wanted to interview his parents all the time. They were media darlings. Matthew had little patience for it.

"And they want to talk to you, too."

This pleased him even less. "And maybe I don't feel like being interviewed," he said.

"Ohhh, Matty," she sighed and sank down onto the bed

next to him. "Are you going to be like this?"

"Like what? I just don't get off on being interviewed the way you and Dad do, that's all."

"It's not a matter of 'getting off' on anything," Carol told him with extreme patience. "It's a matter of doing what's expected. Of doing what's right for people in our social sphere. You understand that, don't you, Matty?"

I understand that I'm sick of being called Matty, went through his mind. He turned to say something to her . . .

But the harshness that was on his lips, and what he was about to say, faded away. Instead he smiled. He actually smiled, which was not something he did all that often. But there was something about his mother—something about the way she acted, about her total devotion to himself and his father—that still touched him, even at this age.

He had little patience for the hypocrisy and stupidity of the world. He didn't put up with it. He didn't have to put up with it. The world acted upon his say-so.

His mother, though, was an original. A rarity.

She was a fascinating dichotomy, almost two different women. At home she would fawn over him, ask him what she could do for him, cater to his every whim. Yet he had had occasion to see her in court, in her environment as a lawyer, and he had been impressed. More than impressed, he'd been knocked out. She had kicked serious ass in court, and if there was one thing that he could empathize with, it was kicking ass. She'd won his admiration that day, and his devotion. For he realized that day that the attention she lavished over him at home was not because she had nothing else to do. It was not because she was some sort of sitcom bubbleheaded mother. It was because she chose to be that way, to care about him to the exclusion of all else at home.

"Yeah . . . sure, Mom, I understand," he said. "Look . . . could you do me one thing, though? In front of the reporters . . . don't call me Matty, okay? I'm eighteen in two days. Call me Matt?"

She smiled at him. "Is it okay if I call you Matty when no one else is around?"

Not really. "Sure," he said.

"Good." She riffled his hair and walked out of the room.

He lay there a moment longer, watching holo-v. Most programs these days were made to play either on the more expensive, fancy home holo-vid sets or on the plain old TV screens that less fortunate individuals had to subsist with. The images were raised off the screen on Matt's holo-v by a good foot or so, and he watched a TV detective deck some crook. Then he got up and went to his window. He stared out at the snow that was falling softly.

"Damnedest thing," he said, and laughed softly to himself.

12

Chuck made sure to grip firmly on to the leash that Rommel was using to "guide" him. As the fake blind man made his way through the lobby of the hotel, the clerks and other people were properly deferential to him. He wondered, if they knew that he wasn't blind, would they then pound him to bits to show their appreciation for his little bit of fakery? Yes, probably they would. He made sure to look neither right nor left as Rommel brought him through.

I still hate this, Rommel told him.

Under his breath, Chuck muttered, "It's not for much longer."

They made it to the outside of the hotel and waited.

The morning before Christmas. Tonight would be Christmas Eve. He thought back on earlier Christmases and somehow, none of them would ever have managed to prepare him for this one.

A chill wind blew through him, and he drew his jacket tighter around himself. The sky was still dark and threatening, and he had the distinct feeling that it was going to start snowing again just about anytime.

Was it really the kid? Was he really causing all this?

The visions of hell and damnation that had leaped through his mind before were still tormenting him. Intellectually, he knew he had to be right. That this kid was a powerful psionic, not some spawn of the devil.

On the other hand, theologians would argue that the powers had to come from *some*where. Of course, the same argument could be made for his powers as well. He'd even felt that way once or twice himself.

The more he thought about meeting young Matthew Olivetti, the more nervous he became.

Through the darkened sunglasses he saw a car pull up, and Rommel started walking toward it. It was a surprisingly large car for today's gas-conscious consumer. On the one hand, he should have been grateful since that meant more than adequate space for Rommel to squeeze his bulk into the back seat. On the other hand, the upstanding environmentalist in him balked at it.

Carmen stepped out and opened the door for him. Rommel slid into the back and Chuck made sure to feel his way before he got in, sliding his hand along the outside of the door frame, just in case somebody was watching.

He realized that Carmen was watching him with open curiosity. "Wanna tell me what's with the act?" she said as he slid into the seat next to her.

"They would've given me problems about Rommel if they'd thought he was anything other than a seeing-eye dog," he replied.

"Oh. I don't see why. If they objected to him, you could have just had him eat them." The car started up and they pulled away.

"Very funny," Chuck said. "Why did we take your car?"

"Because I feel more comfortable in my car, that's why.

Instead of that talking freak show you ride around in. I like being able to drive myself."

He shrugged. "So tell me what the setup is here."

"The setup is that I arranged to interview Carol and Lyle Olivetti. You are my faithful photographer."

"But I don't have a—"

She shoved a camera in his lap. "Now you do. Also, while I talk to the parents, you're going to be the one who talks to Matthew."

"Good plan."

"Yeah, good plan. Except since we know what that kid is capable of, I'm sweating bullets over it."

"He won't try anything while I'm there," said Chuck. "He'll know me for what I am, just as I know him."

She glanced at him. "You actually sound like you might like him or something? Are you out of your mind?"

He shook his head firmly. "I do not 'like him,' as you put it. We're not about to become best buddies. I know what he is, and I know what he's done. At the same time, I have a perspective you don't have. I can see how he got the way he is. I can understand. I can even feel sorry for him. These powers we get—we don't ask for them. We don't even fully comprehend them. It's like . . ." He fished for an analogy and, naturally, came up with sports. "It's as if, when you're a kid in high school, and you play baseball. And they clock your arm at throwing at ninety-nine miles per hour, and accurately. All sorts of attention is lavished on you, people fawn all over you, clubs offer to pay scandalous amounts of money to you. And this high school kid gets completely screwed up."

"Gee, money and adoration—that would screw me right up," said Carmen dryly.

"See? See, that's exactly my point. That's the reaction most people have. The only person who would fully understand what the young pitcher is going through is someone who is, say, already a ballplayer. A top pitcher, who went through the same wringer that the kid is going through. Only he would understand the sorts of pressures that are being put on the kid, and what that can do to your mind."

"And if the kid started throwing fastballs at batters' heads all the time, not caring if he cracked their skulls open like ripe melons?" asked Carmen. "How would the old pro view the young turk then?"

He grimaced. "Probably not very well."

"Uh-huh. My point exactly." She glanced into her rear-view mirror and frowned. "You know, when I watch vids or something, and the cops always look in their mirrors and announce, 'That car is following us,' I always wonder how they spot it with so many cars on the road. How do they pick it out? But here I am, in my car, on the road, and I can tell you that we're being followed."

"Really?" said Chuck, immediately feeling apprehensive. The possibility of the Complex being after him at any time was always a very real one. "How do you know?"

"It's your car."

He craned his neck. "What?"

"And there's no one driving it."

"What?"

She was right. Weaving in and out of traffic behind them was the RAC 3000. There was no one at the wheel.

"Oh, my God," he muttered. "Pull over."

She did so. As he anticipated, the RAC obediently pulled in behind her. Chuck got out of the car and walked back toward his own vehicle. Opening the passenger side door, he stuck his head in.

"You want to tell me what the devil you're doing here?"

"I have always followed you when you go somewhere without me, Charles," said Rac simply. "It's part of my programming."

"Part of your programming?! Lord above, Rac. Should

I be grateful you didn't follow me into my hotel room? Into the bathroom?"

"The dimensions and weight capacity of the elevators would seem to preclude—"

"Never mind," he said. "Look, I'm ordering you to return to the garage you're housed in. The garage! Lord, how did you get out of it! The parking attendants—"

"Are familiar with the RAC 3000 capabilities," replied the car primly—even with a touch of pride. "I inform them of my destination. They simply charge in and out fees to the imprint taken from your Card."

"Nice of them to tell me."

"They assumed you knew."

"Great. Just great. Rac—listen to me. I'm giving you a direct order. Go back to the garage and sit there until I need you. Don't follow me. Don't pursue me. Don't do anything except what I'm telling you, which is 'lay off.' Do we understand each other?"

"Your instructions are quite clear, Charles," she said. She sounded hurt. He'd hurt his car's feelings. This was insane. Next thing he knew, he was going to apologize to his shoes for walking too much in them.

"I do not understand," Rac added, "why you would feel the necessity of riding around in that other vehicle. Have I not been adequate in performing my functions?"

"Yes, more than adequate. Excellent. Exemplary."

"Perhaps the other car is more aesthetic?"

"No! No, it doesn't look better than you."

"Seats are superior?"

"Rac! I don't believe this!" And for emphasis he slammed a fist down on the hood.

"You don't have to hit me, Charles," said Rac.

"Oh, Jesus. Look . . . Rac. It's not you, okay? It's me. It's the kind of guy I am, okay? I like cars that don't talk, okay? Cars that are fast and keep their mouths shut. Cars that don't criticize my taste in music or give me problems about getting into them if I'm scruffy. I just have trouble sticking with any one car, okay? I've never had a really long relationship with a car. Something's always breaking down, and one thing leads to another, and eventually I have trouble putting the brakes on it, or I just can't get it in gear anymore. So I have to scrap the whole thing and start over. What can I tell you, Rac? I'm just one of those guys who likes to ride around."

The car was silent for a long moment.

"I believe you're being sarcastic, Charles."

"Rac, go back to the garage. Now."

"Yes, Charles."

The car turned around and headed back in the direction it had come from. He stood there watched it go, and then returned to Carmen. She was seated in her car, but it was clear from her expression that she had heard the whole thing.

He climbed into the passenger seat and closed the door. "Go ahead," he sighed. "Say it."

She looked at him with disdain. "You slut."

13

"What's that place?" he asked, pointing to a large building. People were bustling in and out of it, many with suitcases. It almost reminded him of an airport.

"You are new in town, aren't you?" she asked. "That's the terminal for the Bullet Train. You know. The high-speed thing that the Japanese put in. San Francisco to New York in two days, on cushions of magnetic force." She shook her head. "Why anyone would take the thing when you can go by plane in just a few hours is beyond me."

He shrugged. "Maybe people who value the concept of just taking things a little easier like to ride it."

"Who knows? Who cares?"

The door of the Olivettis' brownstone opened, and a smiling Carol Olivetti was standing there. She made a sweeping gesture that was in the best style of old-time Hollywood movie stars, and said, "Welcome to our home."

At least that's what she started to say. What she managed to get out was "Wel—" and then her eyes went wide as she saw Rommel.

"Most people have that reaction," said Carmen, and she immediately stuck out a hand. "I'm Carmen Friedman. Good to meet you, Mrs. Olivetti. This is my photographer—"

"Chuck Green," he said quickly, holding on to the false name he'd devised for this little outing.

Carol Olivetti shook his hand, but she had not removed her gaze from the hulking form of Rommel. "What an . . . impressive . . . animal."

"Yes, we're all impressed," said Chuck. "Can't be too careful nowadays."

"No, you can't," agreed Carol Olivetti. "Uhm . . . he's not going to come in here, is he?"

"I'd hate to leave him outside," Chuck told her.

"Last time we did, he ate a construction worker," Carmen added. Chuck fired a glance at her.

Mrs. Olivetti forced a gracious smile. "Of course. Of course. If you assure me he's well trained . . ."

"Ohhhh, he'll be fine." Chuck smiled down at Rommel. "You're not going to cause any problems, are you, boy?" he asked in his most patronizing tone.

Rommel looked up at him. *Get neutered.*

"He'll be fine," Chuck said with certainty.

They walked in and Carmen looked around with unabashed amazement. "This place is gorgeous," she said.

"Decorated everything myself," said Mrs. Olivetti, trying to ignore the clacking of Rommel's toenails on the parquet floor. "Didn't just hire someone to come in and do all the work. I take pride in it."

"I'm sure you do, Mrs. Olivetti," said Carmen.

"Please, call me Carol."

"Certainly, Carol. And you can call me Ms. Friedman."

Carol blinked in confusion, and seeing that she wasn't getting it, Carmen quickly said, "No, please. I was kidding. Call me Carmen."

"Carmen." Mrs. Olivetti looked slightly relieved. "You know, I know I've seen your name on stories. Usually they're of national importance or some such. I would imagine that stories about us would be more appropriate for . . . I don't know . . . the life-styles section or something."

"Oh, you and your husband are definitely national figures," said Carmen.

"And Matthew. Don't forget Matthew," said Carol, holding up a mock-scolding finger.

"Oh, we couldn't forget Matthew," said Chuck. "Not for a moment."

"Come. Let me give you the nickel tour, as we used to say," said Carol. She glanced at Carmen's black leather shoulder bag. "That looks heavy. Can I take that for you?"

"No, I'm fine," said Carmen, patting it. "Just fine."

They followed her through the house, Chuck trying to pay attention to the various things that she was pointing out. It had little relevance or interest for him. Instead he was concerned with the almost suffocating feeling of power that seemed to throb throughout the entire house.

He's here, said Rommel. *I feel him.*

"Me, too," muttered Chuck.

Carol Olivetti, who had just been raving about some painting hanging on the wall of the study they'd entered, turned to Chuck in delight. "Oh, you're an art buff, too, Mr. Green?"

"Chuck. Oh, yeah . . ." he said, not having really heard what she was saying, but not wishing to let on.

"Tell me . . . what do you think of Raphael?"

He frowned. "He was some sort of turtle, wasn't he?"

Carol stared at him for a moment, and then laughed delightedly. "Oh, you journalism people. Now you're making jokes, right?"

Chuck laughed agreeably. "Oh, yeah, we wild and wacky journalists."

"So tell me," said Carmen Friedman quickly. "Where

are all the servants? Don't tell me you clean up the place, in addition to doing the decorating."

"Oh, no certainly not. I mean, not that I couldn't. But with my schedule, it would be impossible. We gave our people the week off, though. It is Christmas, after all."

"Absolutely," said Carmen. "Absolutely."

"Lyle!" she called out. "Lyle, come out here, please! Matthew! The company is here!"

They walked up to a room where the heavy oaken door was closed. Mrs. Olivetti rapped on it with authority, keeping a gracious smile on her face. "Not now, dammit!" called out an angry voice from within.

The smile remained on her face, but now there was annoyance touching her eyes. "Lyle," she said firmly, the gracious hostess demeanor slipping away, "we have guests. We discussed this, remember?"

"Don't bother me with this bullshit. I'm on the phone."

Her hand rested on the doorknob a moment, and then she seemed to think better of what was occurring to her. "It'll just be a minute or two," she told them.

"Be a hell of a lot longer than that," Lyle's voice came from inside.

Chuck watched her carefully as the blood seemed to drain from Carol Olivetti's face. She banged firmly on the door and said, "Lyle . . . open this right now. Or I'll turn the dog loose." She was looking with significance at Chuck.

"Dog? What dog? What the hell are you talking about? Can't I even conduct a simple call without—"

Chuck was beginning to lose patience. Not to mention that he was feeling embarrassment on her behalf.

"Rommel," he said softly. "Announce yourself."

Rommel barked. Once. That was all that was needed, as the bark echoed off the polished walls and parquet floors.

There was the sound of running feet, and the door was yanked open. Lyle Olivetti stood there, staring, appalled, at the monster that was in front of him. He pointed a wavering finger. "What the hell is that?"

"My new friend," his wife informed him, smiling sweetly. "Lyle, say hello to our guests."

Lyle couldn't take his eyes off Rommel. "Hello," he said numbly.

Chuck looked from husband to wife, and immediately intuited that all was not well.

"Shall we go in?" said Carol suavely, with a wave of her arm. Lyle nodded and went back into the den. Friedman and Chuck started to follow them in, when suddenly Chuck stiffened. Rommel growled low in his throat, a noise that caused both of the Olivettis to stop and turn in alarm.

"It's okay."

The calm words had been spoken by Matthew.

He stood on the upper landing, looking down at them, like a god from on high.

"Oh! Matthew," said Carol. "These are the reporters I told you about. This is Miss Carmen Friedman, and this is Mr. Chuck Green. Oh, and this . . . Rommel, was it?"

"Yes," said Chuck tonelessly. "Rommel. Rommel," and the second time it was with a bit of warning to it.

"Say hello to the young man."

Let me kill him now.

In a voice so low as to be practically inaudible, Chuck murmured, "I doubt you can," and then louder, "Come on, Rommel. Say hello."

Rommel barked once more, and if a dog's bark could be said to be laced with anger, Rommel's most definitely was.

"Shall we go and chat?" said Carol Olivetti, gesturing to the den.

"Mother," said Matthew, not having moved from his spot, "why don't Mr. Green and I talk up here, while you chat with Ms. Friedman."

Carol looked from one to the other. "Well, now, I don't think that . . ."

"Good idea," Chuck said tonelessly. And then, with re-inforced vigor, he said, "I think that would be a very good idea. Don't you, Carmen?"

"Oh, yes," she said. She was staring at Matthew with a sense of . . . what? Fear? Awe? Some of both? "Yes, why don't we do that. We're all busy people. This will give us a chance to cover some of the same ground at the same time. Yes, let's do that."

Chuck started up the stairs, Rommel behind him.

"The dog stays down there," Matthew said firmly.

Rommel growled, but all Chuck said was, "Rommel, stay."

He wants to get you alone.

Chuck patted Rommel's head. "I'll be fine."

You'll be dead.

"I mean it, Rommel. Stay."

Chuck climbed the stairs, taking them with measured tread. Not too fast, not too slow. The stairs went up at a long, lazy curve and gave Chuck plenty of time to assess what he was facing.

Not *what,* he scolded himself furiously. Who. This was still a human being, not some hell-spawned demon.

At least, that's what Chuck was going to keep telling himself, and hope that he wasn't wrong.

He got to the top of the landing. Matthew hadn't moved from the spot. Power seemed to radiate from him, and an aura of confidence that was overpowering. He stood, not like a teenager, but like someone who was much, much older.

Matthew stuck out a hand, and Chuck took it firmly.

"It's a pleasure to meet at last," said Matthew softly.

"At last?" replied Chuck. "You make it sound as if we're old friends."

"Ohhh, in a way," said Matthew. "In a way, we are."

From below, Carol Olivetti said, "Now why don't you

two go off and chat, and if we need you to come down-stairs for something, we'll be sure to call you."

"That would be fine, Mother," said Matthew, but all the time he was staring at Chuck. It was as if his eyes were trying to bore their way into the back of Chuck's head.

Matthew stepped back and made a sweeping gesture. "Won't you come into my parlor?"

"Said the spider to the fly?" asked the Psi-Man.

"I've always liked that poem," replied the Chaos Kid.

14

Matthew stepped back and allowed Chuck to enter. "This is my room. How do you like it?" There was quiet amusement in his voice.

Chuck looked around it. "Nice room. Typical teenager's room, although a bit more austere than others."

"What did you expect? Rock and roll posters on the wall?" scoffed Matthew. He closed the door softly behind him and leaned against it.

Chuck nodded slowly and then turned to face him. He held up his camera. "Mind if I take a picture?"

"Go ahead."

Matthew raised a disdainful eyebrow, his arms folded, and Chuck took the shot. He took a second, just to play it safe . . . but play it safe for what? This was all an act. He wasn't really a photographer. And the kid wasn't . . . what? Really a kid?

"So," said Chuck, leaning against a wall. "Tell me about yourself. About what it's like growing up in a family like this."

"It has its moments," said Matthew. He regarded Chuck thoughtfully. "You meet some of the most interesting people. Like . . . priests."

"Priests," said Chuck tonelessly.

"Yes. It's a funny thing about priests. They act like spiritual advisers and such things. But then they turn around, and they spy on you."

Chuck said nothing for a moment. "Spy," he said.

"Hard to believe, isn't it?"

"Very hard."

"I'm going to be eighteen tomorrow," said Matthew, walking halfway around the room and sitting, very straight and tall, on the edge of the bed.

"You having a party?" Chuck asked.

"Oh, yes. A big party."

"Who's invited?"

"The whole city." He smiled. "Everyone can participate. Everyone can be a part of it. There'll be dancing and screaming—"

"Screaming?"

Matthew inclined his head slightly. "Did I say screaming? I meant singing. There will be singing. Of course there will be singing. How could I have meant anything else?"

"You might have," said Chuck slowly, "if you knew a reason why people might start to scream."

"Now why do people scream?"

Chuck was certain that the temperature in the room had gone up since he'd entered. He pulled slightly at his collar. "Because they're afraid of something."

"That's what I think," said Matthew. "I think the exact same thing. Fear. Fear would do it to them. But what would people have to be afraid of on the happiest day of the year? On the birthday of our savior?"

"I don't know. Why don't you tell me?"

Matthew smiled again. It was not a facial gesture that encouraged any sort of positive feelings.

"You know . . . I think I will," said Matthew.

• • •

Carol Olivetti's eyes opened wide. "Lyle," she said slowly, "what do you mean, you're not going to be spending Christmas with us? We're your family! We're the most important thing in your life."

"Look," and he gestured toward Carmen. "I really don't want to discuss this with her sitting here."

"No, we will discuss it!" she said sharply, the facade of gracious—and even slightly empty-headed—hostess slipping away from her. In its place was the hard-edged lawyer who judges and opposing attorneys were accustomed to seeing.

Carmen was looking from one to the other, her recorder whirring. She had not expected this at all. All she had asked was a simple, innocuous opening question: "How are you folks planning to spend the holiday?" Carol had started to launch into a lengthy speech about how they would be spending it together, relaxing in front of a roaring fire, acting like a family out of a Rockwell painting. And then, to her shock, Lyle had promptly disagreed, saying instead that he had to go to New York, and that he was planning to depart on the Bullet Train on Christmas Day.

"But . . . but," she stammered, "what's in New York?"

He was silent for a long moment, and somehow Carmen—who had merely walked into the middle of this—got the distinct feeling that she knew what was coming.

Again he said, "Look, with this reporter here it's not the best time to—"

"Screw her!" shouted Carol. "You tell me, Lyle, and you tell me right now!"

He looked at her evenly, his sharp gaze not faltering, and then he said, "All right. All right, Carol. You push this, you insist on discussing this now. Give the world a firsthand scoop on our life. That's your way, isn't it. That's what you love. Your name in the paper, the world-class ego. All right, you've got it. You have fucking got it. I'm leaving you, Carol. Happy now?"

Carol Olivetti blanched. However, still in total control, she did not make any effort to articulate a word before she had her thoughts fully formed. When she spoke, her voice was low and deadly. "It's for her, isn't it?"

He genuinely looked surprised. "For who? What are you—"

"That little model with the sweet little ass, right, Lyle?" She looked triumphant at his discomfiture. "What, you thought I didn't know about her? You thought I'm not aware of your every move. That little bitch—"

"You keep Sandy out of it," said Lyle Olivetti sharply.

"Sandy. Yes." She turned to Carmen. "Sandy Sendak. Remember, you heard her name here first, Carmen. I daresay you'll be hearing it a great deal. You'll probably even be typing it quite a few times. She'll go from being a second-rate model to a first-rate media siren. That's how these things work. All you have to do is be screwing around with a world-famous real-estate dealer."

Carmen couldn't believe it. "You—you guys are really serious about this. This isn't just some sort of setup to scam a reporter."

But she saw the way they were looking at each other. There was too much fury flowing between the two of them. This wasn't an act. This was just incredible timing.

"Yes, I think I will tell you," said Matthew. "Because there's not a lot you can do about it."

He was studying Chuck very closely, as if examining a worm under a microscope. "Tell me first, though . . . what do you think of me?"

"What do I think?" said Chuck. He smiled thinly, and kept telling himself that this was a kid. This was only a kid. "I think that you are a very disturbed young man."

"Really?"

"I think you are very bright, and very talented . . . and

you think that you are even more bright and talented than you already are. I think that you feel as if you're on top of the world, and are going to stay there."

"Really?" he said again.

Chuck nodded.

"So tell me," said Matthew, "are we going to just keep dicking around here, or are we going to get to it."

"It's your house," Chuck told him. "I just want to be polite. That's what my mother always taught me. Did your mother teach you anything? About manners? About the sanctity of life?"

"Don't yammer on to me about sanctity of life," Matthew said sharply. "I know all about it. I know all about people. I know what they do to people who are different, which means that people who are different have to do it first."

"People who are different," said Chuck, "who are better . . . they have a responsibility to others. If they are superior, they have a moral obligation to help those who are lesser than themselves."

"Oh, really?" laughed Matthew. "So, humans are superior to cattle, and chickens. Are we supposed to be using our superior intellect for the betterment of cattle and chickens everywhere? Or do we use that beloved intellect to find new and more efficient ways to breed them faster, and kill them faster, so that we can eat them faster."

"That's somewhat different."

"It's no different. Predator and prey. The greater stamps upon the lesser. That's life, Mr. Green. That's history. That's evolution. Nature creates the next order to step upon the lesser order, to achieve its rightful place in the grand scheme of things."

He got up from his bed and crossed the room quickly to Chuck. Matthew placed a hand on the wall just to the right of Chuck's head and spoke in a quick, hushed voice.

"Don't tell me," said Matthew, "that you don't give any thought to the place of superior beings in a superior world.

That you don't realize that truly superior people have an obligation, not to their inferiors but to other superior people."

"Might makes right? Is that it?"

"You bet your ass that's it."

Chuck looked him in the eyes. "Have you read Orwell? George Orwell? *1984.*"

"Of course," said Matthew.

"Remember what he said about the future of man, being a boot stomping on your face, forever?"

"Yes. Glorious imagery, isn't it?" Matthew said. "If you happen to be wearing the boot, that is."

"And you feel that you've got the boots right now."

"You bet I've got the boot," said Matthew in a husky voice. "And I'm going to use it."

"Even if it costs lives."

"Even if? That's the point, Green, old bean. What good is having power over life and death if you can't exercise it every now and then."

"Because might makes right?"

"That's it."

Chuck drew himself up to his full height, which was only a shade taller than Matthew. Involuntarily, Matthew took a step back. "And what happens when you run into someone mightier than you?"

"Then that would make him righter."

"Matthew—I want to help you," said Chuck, but there was no sound of pleading in his voice. Instead he spoke with quiet urgency. "I think you're sick."

Matthew thumped on his chest. "Nope. Never felt healthier."

"Not that kind of sick. Sick as in you have no sense of morals. You have no sense of goodness or decency. You think you can do anything."

"See, that's where the basic difference comes in, Chuck," said Matthew. "I don't think that. I know that.

And there's nothing that you, or your damned dog, can do to stop me."

Chuck reached out with his mind, an invisible fist closing around Matthew's chest. The teen gasped as he was lifted off his feet and slammed up against the ceiling.

"I wouldn't bet on that," said Chuck tersely.

And suddenly the temperature around Chuck skyrocketed. Within seconds he was being buffeted by staggering waves of heat that knocked the air out of him and caused him to lose his concentration. Matthew thudded to the bed, the springs protesting under him.

The two of them were momentarily choking, both trying to reestablish their equilibrium. And then Matthew managed to say, "I would bet on that. I'd bet it all on that. And I would win. You hear me, Chuck? I would win."

"Or we would both win," Chuck got out. "Which means we would both lose."

"I haven't done anything," said Matthew. "Not that you could prove. Going to tell the police? Tell my parents? They'll laugh in your face. Only thing you could possibly do, Chuck, is try to kill me in cold blood. You got the stones for that?"

Chuck stood, having recovered his breath. He glared at Matthew for a moment, and then headed for the door.

"Battle lines have been drawn, Chuck," called out Matthew, his dark eyes flashing. "We know where each of us stands. But I'll warn you about one thing, Chuck. You have no idea what you're fucking with."

Chuck paused at the door, then turned and glanced back at Matthew. "Neither do you," he said.

"This interview is over," said Lyle. He stood and approached Carmen with a no-nonsense attitude.

"This interview will be over when I say it's over," Carol said angrily, but her husband was paying her no mind. He grabbed Carmen by the upper arm.

"Hey!" said Carmen. "Get your hands off me! I don't care how much money you've got!"

He hauled her to her feet and she yanked away from him. "Hey, I was ready to do a nice, fashionable puff piece about successful people," said Carmen, stabbing a finger at them. "The two of you decided to turn it into divorce court."

"He started it!" said Carol, the specter of bad publicity now hovering before her eyes. "Carmen, certainly you see that. I didn't want this to happen."

"What I see is two pathetic people who have a lot of shit to work out, and you'll excuse me if I don't hang around to watch it." She spun on her heel and walked out of the den.

She walked out into the main foyer and Chuck was just coming down the long winding stairs. She'd been so pre-occupied with the unexpected nonsense of the parents that she'd almost forgotten the main purpose of their coming there.

Something was definitely off with Chuck. He looked like he'd been through a war. His hair was disheveled, and the edges of his beard looked—what? Singed? Could that be? How on earth . . .

Rommel was waiting for him at the bottom of the stairs, and Chuck walked past him, straight to Carmen. "I have to talk to his parents," he said tersely.

"Forget it," said Carmen. "Let's go."

"They have to know!"

"They're not going to believe you!" she said, holding him firmly by the shoulders. He was passingly surprised at the strength in her grip and her ability to restrain him, despite the fact that she only came to midway up his chest. "Something went wrong. They're having all kinds of marital problems. Now is not the time to tell them, 'Oh, by the way. Your kid is a corrupt psionic murderer.' "

"I can't just stand by and—"

"It won't accomplish anything, dammit!" she snarled,

pulling on his arm. She heard a low, threatening growl from Rommel, but she took her life in her hands and ignored it. "We'll come back in a day or so. We'll tell them then. Nothing's going to happen in a day or so."

"I wouldn't stake my life on that."

She was dragging him toward the front door. Now Chuck could make out the sounds of raised, angry voices coming from the den. She was right. They were going at it like two gladiators. Invective and bile being thrown around that could only come as a result of love gone sour. If their words had been acid, both their bodies would be scarred and burning right now.

"I still think I should—"

"Don't think," she said, pulling him with determination. "You only run into problems when you think. Come *on!*"

She got him to the front door and started to shove him out. The last thing he caught a glimpse of was Matthew Olivetti, standing there on the landing, smiling down in that maddeningly superior way he had. Then he was out the door.

Rommel was following them as they headed for Carmen's car. "Tell me about the kid," she said urgently.

"Utterly confident. Utterly in control. Certain that he's on top of the world and owns it, too. Frankly, I couldn't say he's completely wrong." They got in the car, Rommel squeezing himself in.

Carmen was moving with a determined speed that made it seem as if demons were on her heels. She was clearly anxious to put as much distance between herself and the house as possible. Chuck couldn't blame her. And yet . . .

The car started to roll forward and Chuck said firmly, "Stop the car."

"Forget it."

"Stop it!" he said, and telekinetically slammed down the brake pedal. The car screeched to a halt and was almost rear-ended by another car. The other car swerved around them and sped off, honking, with the driver flipping an obscene gesture.

"I'm going back in."

She paled. "You don't want to do that. Trust me."

Inside the house, Carol Olivetti was circling the couch like a tigress, informing her husband of just what he had let himself in for. Then the toe of her foot tapped against something. She looked down.

"Oh, great," she said. "Carmen left her bag here."

"Who gives a shit!" Lyle said angrily. "If it weren't for that bitch coming here, our personal business wouldn't be spread all over tomorrow's newspaper!"

"Fuck you, Lyle!"

"Yeah," said Lyle, with the sort of relish that can only be had when one is about to say something that one knows is really going to hurt the feelings of another. "Yeah, well, if there'd been more of that at home, I wouldn't have had to go elsewhere for it."

Her cheeks stung as if she'd been slapped. Then, with a slow smile, she replied, "May I say that the same goes double for me."

It took him a moment to understand what she was saying, and while he did, she picked up the case and started for the door. Then he fully comprehended. "You're lying!" he shouted.

"You wish," she retorted.

He came right after her, shouting at her with mounting fury. She took cold comfort in ignoring him as she went out the door, clutching the case in her hand.

He followed her into the foyer, and Matthew was looking down at them.

She turned on her husband furiously and said, "Shut up! Shut up! Matthew should not be subjected to this!"

Matthew looked at them in confusion. "What? What do you—"

"You mean he shouldn't find out about his mother, the whore?" snapped Lyle Olivetti.

Matthew's eyes opened wide. He knew his parents had been having problems, but they'd usually managed to put on a good, even entertaining display of parental devotion. It was obvious now that the curtain was coming down on that particular show.

"I said shut up!" she snarled. "I want to try to catch Carmen and give her her bag back."

"Fine! Fine!" said Lyle. "Worry more about the reporter than—"

Something warned Matthew. He didn't know what, or how. But suddenly the world seemed to iris out, and all his senses focused in on the nondescript black case that was in his mother's hand.

"Mom!" he shouted. "Get rid of—!"

"Get rid of what!" shouted his father. "Get rid of the old man? Is that what you're going to say, you ingra—"

Then there was a flash of light that seemed to swallow the entire world.

"I've got to go back in!" said Chuck with more urgency. "I can't just walk away from them! They've got to know what they've got for a son, no matter how much convincing it takes. Even if they don't believe, at least I'll have tried."

He threw open the car door and jumped out. Rommel was right behind him, shoving his way out from the back seat.

"Chuck, no!" shouted Carmen. "Don't go in there! You can't!"

He stopped a moment and turned. "I have to. It's who I am."

"It's who you *won't* be, namely Chuck Simon! Don't go in there, I mean it! It's settled, Chuck. It's over! Don't you understand? Do I have to goddamn spell it out for you? *It's over!*"

He frowned. "What in the world are you talking about?"

And the house exploded.

15

The next thing Chuck knew, his face was wet, and there were sirens screaming all around him.

The air was filled with an acrid stench. Slowly Chuck opened his eyes and saw Rommel staring at him.

"What . . . happened?" he managed to get out, and he started to sit up.

Immediately a voice shouted from nearby, "Sir, don't sit up! We'll have the ambulance for you in a second!"

He looked down and saw that he was on a stretcher. "What happened?" he said again, trying to assemble his scrambled thoughts.

The house blew up, Rommel told him.

"You're kidding."

You didn't do it?

"Of course not!"

Too bad. I thought you were finally going for the direct approach.

He put a hand to the side of his head, and came away with sticky redness on his fingers. "I'm bleeding."

You're observant today.

"Let's get out of here."

Chuck staggered to his feet, and immediately a paramedic was there. A young blond man who had not just nearly been blown to bits, as a result, was somewhat more refreshed than Chuck. "Sir, please," he said, but it was clear from his tone that it wasn't a request. "You could have a concussion, you could be in shock. Please just stay here and the ambulance will be along in a moment. The one that I came with just took away Mr. Olivetti's body."

"I have to go," said Chuck tonelessly.

"Sir, I must insist . . ."

Chuck smiled at him mirthlessly. "My insistence is bigger than yours. Rommel: insist for me."

Rommel growled in no uncertain terms at the paramedic.

The paramedic stepped back, immediately and understandably intimidated by the big dog. Chuck leaned on Rommel with one hand and walked away, limping slightly. The paramedic did nothing to challenge them.

Chuck stared at the smoking ruins of a building. All over there were holo-vid news cameras, police trying to push people back, fire engines, reporters . . .

Reporters.

"Carmen?" he said, and then louder, "Carmen!"

She's not here.

"Where is she?"

She drove off right after the building blew. You got hit by some flying rubble and went down. A police car was passing by, so that's how there was so much activity so fast. It only happened a little while ago.

"She—she didn't try to help me?"

Maybe the police scared her off.

"But why?" said Chuck in confusion. "Why would . . ."

And then the haze of his befuddlement started to dispel, and he remembered her shouting a warning. A warning about the building about to blow up. She had known. She had . . .

"My God," he whispered, "she set it. She set the bomb."

He heard an uproar behind him and turned. The rescue teams had managed to clear away some of the rubble. They were bringing out, on a stretcher, the mangled body of Carol Olivetti. It was painfully obvious that she was dead. Excavation was still going on to relocate the remains of the rest of her family.

"You!" Someone was shouting to him and Chuck now saw that the paramedic had summoned a police officer, who was approaching Chuck and gesturing to him.

"I can't go to a hospital," Chuck said firmly to Rommel. "They'll ID me."

Fine. I'll kill the policeman.

"You can't."

Okay. You kill him. I'll kill the other idiot.

That's when there was the roar of a familiar engine, and the gleaming red RAC 3000 shot up alongside Chuck and Rommel. The door flew open and Chuck leaped in, Rommel at his side. The police officer shouted for them to halt, and the car paid them no mind as it roared off with its fugitive cargo.

"Rac! I told you specifically not to follow me!" said Chuck. "I told you to return to the garage."

"Of course you did, Charles," said Rac reasonably. "But my main programming is to care for my driver. Your best interests will be served by . . ."

"But you're making value judgments! That's ridiculous! You're a machine!"

"So is a human being," replied Rac. "We both have brains based in electrical impulses. We both have parts that our brains instruct."

"Humans have souls!"

"Humans have souls because humans have assigned themselves souls," said Rac reasonably. "If I said I had a soul, my claim would be no less valid than yours, and no more provable."

"But humans make machines!"

"Who made you?"

"Well . . ." He paused. "My parents."

"Humans."

"Presumably," he admitted. "But—but humans can reprogram machines."

Rac turned a corner with a squealing of tires and said calmly, "When you do it to machines, it's called reprogramming. When you do it to other humans, it's called brainwashing. You're arguing semantics with me, Charles, and I can recite the entire Oxford unabridged dictionary. Can you?"

"No," he muttered.

"So there you are. Be honest, Charles . . . the only difference between humans and machines is that humans believe that they are more than they are. That doesn't make you better. Just pretentious."

What's going on?

"Rac is saying that a machine is as good as a human being."

I wouldn't say that.

"Thanks, Rommel."

Dogs are better than humans, though.

Chuck sighed. "I'm arguing with my dog and my car. And they're winning. This isn't a life. This is Kafka."

16

Chuck staggered in through the hotel lobby, leaning heavily on Rommel. He did not have his sunglasses, or Rommel's muzzle (which didn't upset Rommel one bit). As a result he had to work hard at disfocusing his eyes when the desk clerk came briskly around the desk and went to Chuck, concern etched on his face.

"Mr. Green, what happened?" he asked.

Deciding not to needlessly complicate matters, Chuck said—with more fogginess in his voice than he really felt—"Mugged. Some men . . . I don't know how many . . ."

The desk clerk made sharp, *tsk* noises. "Attacking a blind man. How low will some people stoop!"

"Beats me," said Chuck.

"Look at your head . . . oh, I'm sorry. I didn't mean to say look."

Chuck actually grimaced a smile at that. " 'Look' and 'see' aren't dirty words. Don't take things so literally."

The desk clerk smiled at that, although Chuck made

certain not to look directly at it. "Yes, indeed, you're right. Jack! I'm calling for the bellman," he told Chuck.

"That won't be necess—"

"See that Mr. Green gets up to his room," said the desk clerk. The bellman, a skinny, pimply kid, looked nervously at Rommel.

"Really, you don't have to do that," Chuck told him.

"I insist, sir. I really do," said the desk clerk firmly.

"There's nothing more to say on the matter. Jack," he added, and then gestured silently that Jack was to do as instructed. "Mr., Green, I'll arrange for the house physician to see to that nasty head wound. I'll also call the police—"

"Pointless," said Chuck. "The people who did it never spoke. I have no way of identifying them. As soon as I get to my room I'll call and have my Card deactivated so they can't run charges up on it. Other than that, there's nothing more to do."

"I don't understand, though, how they incapacitated your dog. A sizable creature like that . . ."

"Mace," said Chuck quickly. "They shot it in his face before we knew what was happening."

The desk clerk winced at that, and then he frowned. "At least they missed your necklace."

"Oh. This." Chuck's hand reached up automatically to feel the spoon that hung from a chain around his neck, bent by the power of his mind into a stylized "A." "A for Anna. First name of my ex-wife. I guess an old spoon wasn't of interest to them. Just has sentimental value, really."

The desk clerk gave a slight bow. "I suppose you have to take the good things where you can find them, sir."

Some minutes later the house doctor was finishing the bandages on Chuck's head. She was a prematurely gray-haired woman with a no-nonsense air about her. "Any dizziness? Vomiting or nausea?" Chuck shook his head.

"Still," she said, "I'd like you to go to a hospital and have it x-rayed. You can't be too careful in the cases of head wounds."

"I appreciate your concern, Doctor, but I'll be fine. Really."

She eyed him skeptically, and then suddenly brought a probe up and flashed it in Chuck's face. He flinched automatically at the bright light. "Some blind man," she said.

"Look, uhm," Chuck began.

She held up a hand. "I don't give a damn what your story is. It's not illegal to pretend you're blind. Your reasons are of no interest to me."

"You going to tell the desk clerk?"

"Not unless he asks me. My services will appear on your hotel bill. I don't suggest you read it too closely. Might give yourself away," she added dryly.

"Yes, ma'am."

After she left, he went to the bathroom mirror and checked his face over. Then he sat on the edge of the bathtub and stared into space.

Carmen had set the bomb. There was no longer any doubt in his mind on that. But why? Why had she done such a thing?

Was she that afraid of Matthew Olivetti?

He got up and went to the TV. Upon turning it on, he was faced with the area that he had just left. A newsman was reporting on the mysterious bombing that had taken the lives of millionaire realtor Lyle Olivetti and his family. He sat there and watched the unmoving form of Matthew Olivetti being pulled from the rubble and put onto a stretcher. Several other pedestrians were also reported dead or critically injured.

He leaned back and sighed. Well . . . it was over. For better or worse, the threat that Matthew Olivetti posed was definitely over. His crimes had been paid for.

Now he had to find the woman who had committed a crime in order to achieve that payment.

He picked up the phone, prepared to dial her newspaper, and then stopped. Perhaps she thought him dead. She probably did. In which case, why alert her to the fact that he was alive? If he was dead, she was in the clear. There was no one else who could possibly connect her with what had just happened.

He had to find out. He had to go and talk with her.

He had the bellman bring up from the gift shop a spare pair of sunglasses, and equipped once more with a disguise capable of fooling anyone except a medically trained individual, Chuck went back out. He paused only once, to assure the desk clerk that he was on his way over to the hospital to get his head x-rayed. Moments later he was in the RAC 3000, the door slamming securely behind him. Rommel drew his tail in quickly, narrowly missing have the door shut on it.

"Where to, Charles?" Rac asked politely.

"The *Tribune*," was the brisk reply.

"I'll drive," Rac told him. "Your head was recently injured. You can't do anything too strenuous."

"Fine. Fine."

You're letting the car drive again?

"Yes, I'm letting the car drive again," Chuck sighed. "Give it a rest, okay, Rommel?"

Drop me off up ahead.

Chuck shook his head. "For a dog that scares the daylights out of everyone else, it's amazing how much grief you give me over this."

Rommel growled sullenly.

Once again Chuck left Rommel down in the lobby of the *Tribune* building, under the uncomfortable eye of the guard in the front. As he rode the elevator up, he went over in his mind what he would say to Carmen. What could he say? *Hi, you bombed the Olivettis' house. You killed them. How could you do that?* Oh, that was going to be a wonderful approach. Mister Cool.

He stepped off and glanced around. The maze of office cubicles confronted him once more, and his sense of direction was momentarily thrown. The elevator doors slid shut behind him.

"Mr. Green!"

He turned and saw Erwin, the guy who Carmen had called the government editor—the censor—was hailing him like a long-lost pal. It immediately made the hair on the back of Chuck's neck rise. "What can I do for you, Mr. Erwin?" asked Chuck cautiously.

"You're here to see our Miss Friedman, I take it," he said.

"That's right. Is she in?"

"Yes, she is. Right this way."

Chuck frowned but followed him. "You're being terribly cooperative, Mr. Erwin," he couldn't help but observe.

"Oh, just being careful, Mr. Green," said Erwin, walking a few paces ahead with confidence. "Every so often we wind up having people wandering around up here. Makes things uncomfortable and confusing. We try to avoid that. Since I can vouch for you, I'm more than happy to bring you straight to her."

They rounded a corner and Erwin gestured toward an office. "Right this way," he said.

But it was a glass-enclosed wall office, not the cubicle of Carmen Friedman. Now there was a definite buzz of danger in the back of Chuck's mind, and it was edging its way farther forward every moment. "What's this all about?" he demanded. "This isn't Carmen's office."

"Everything will be explained to you," said Erwin, the cloak of politeness slipping away.

Chuck started to back up and then he suddenly spun. The other three editors from the government desk were now coming toward him, and they had guns out. They were clearly ready to use them.

And suddenly a cloth was clapped over his mouth. His eyes opened wide as Erwin muttered, "This won't hurt you, Mr. Simon. It will just put you to sleep, and then the people from the Complex will be here in short order to pick you up."

Idiot! Idiot! Chuck screamed in his mind as the world started to turn into a darkened haze around him.

17

Gil Irvin, who had, mere days before, been scalded nearly to death in the boy's shower room at school, and now was lying in his hospital bed staring up at the TV, felt a sense of wonderment rushing through him.

Bandaged burns covered seventy-five percent of his body. Even with modern skin graft techniques, it would still be months before the injured teen was fully functional again, and even then he would never be his old self. Still, the constant dull, thudding pain that had been his continual companion for hours—even in his sleep—were all forgotten. Everything was forgotten, except the images that he was seeing upon the screen.

The home that slimeball, Matthew Olivetti, lived in— a pile of smoking rubble. There were pictures of the deceased, flashing on the screen. Some old picture of Matthew was flickering there, right after photos of his obnoxious father and equally offensive mother. Dead. All dead.

It had happened a few hours ago. This was perfect. This was absolutely perfect.

Gil Irvin had been of the firm opinion that somehow, in some way, Matthew Olivetti had been responsible for what had happened to him. There was no way to prove it. There was no way to convince anyone of it. But he was certain of it, just the same.

And now . . . now he was gone. What goes around comes around. All was just. All the scores were settled.

He had to see it.

Gil knew, with pure unbridled certainty, that he had to see the body. He had to revel in it. He had to enjoy it, see the ruined corpse, because he knew that he wouldn't be able to get to the funeral. And standing in front of a grave in a few weeks just wouldn't be the same.

Every muscle screaming in protest, every inch of skin a pin-cushioned ache, Gil slowly sat up. It was the most physical activity he'd performed in days, but he had to do it. He almost passed out sitting on the edge of the bed, but something within him wouldn't let him stop.

He had to see it.

Had to see it.

Because somehow, it was more than just reveling in it. Somehow, he didn't fully believe it. He had to see the body to satisfy his own—what? Paranoia? What was it about Olivetti that made it seem as if he could transcend death?

The cold fingers of doubt played about Gil's spine, and propelled the youth up off his sickbed. He knew, beyond any doubt, that the bodies would be here, in the hospital. It was the nearest place. Probably in a few hours, the bodies would be picked up and transported down to the city morgue or something. Or maybe to a funeral home. Who knew? All he knew for sure was that if Matthew Olivetti was downstairs with a tag on his toe, he had to see it.

The only other patient in Gil's room was asleep, snoring softly. The newscast had moved on to other matters, matters of no relevance to Gil. All that mattered was getting out of the room and downstairs without drawing any notice.

His head was virtually the only part of him unbandaged. The moment the water had started to scald him, one hand had gone down reflexively to protect his genitals, and his other arm had flown up to cover his face. Even while writhing on the floor, that's how he continued to shield himself. So after he had now staggered to the closet and pulled on the bathrobe that his parents had brought him, he didn't look—to the undiscerning eye— quite as bad as he actually was.

Every motion that was required to pull on the bathrobe was agonizing, but after his first outcry he chomped down on his lower lip until it bled, rather than take the chance of alerting anyone. His breath came in short, ragged bursts, and he stayed absolutely motionless until he was certain he could deal with the pain.

Why was he putting himself through this?

Because he had to know. Really know, beyond any shadow of a doubt. He had to touch the cold face, stare into the dead eyes.

He knew. He knew Matthew was responsible. And he knew something else . . . that if Matthew were still alive, then he, Gil, would be dead before very long.

He had wanted to talk to Bill Tyler about it. But he had no phone by his bed, and his parents had told him—with artificial smiles pasted on their faces—that Bill couldn't make it over to come and visit him. He wondered what that was all about, but decided that he would think about it later. Right now, Matthew was all that mattered.

His body stiff, Gil made it out into the hallway. He glanced right and left, and did not see the duty nurse around. So frequently there was never a nurse around when he wanted one. Well, now he didn't want one and, luckily, she still wasn't around.

He walked with slow, deliberate steps toward the elevator. He tried to look as nonchalant as possible. Fortunately things were slow at the moment on his floor. There was hardly anyone around. An orderly went by, pushing a mop, and barely acknowledged Gil with a slight inclination of the head. Gil grunted back.

Moments later he made it to an elevator and was leaning against the wall, having pushed the button for the lowest level. He had a feeling that's where it would be. Certainly that's where it always was in all the holo-vid medical shows.

The elevator stopped on one level and two orderlies wheeled in a patient on a gurney. They didn't so much as glance at Gil. The level below that, the doors opened and the patient was wheeled out again. Gil was alone in the elevator.

The doors didn't open again until the bottom floor and Gil stepped out, his slippers slapping against his bare feet.

He followed the signs, and felt a gradual chill in the air that cut through the bandages and into his skin. Although each step was painful for him, it was secondary to the excitement that was building in him.

Matthew Olivetti's body. Deadface Matthew, a stiff at last. He, Gil, had the last laugh. It was wonderful.

He peered in through the swinging doors of the morgue. He saw a couple of bodies lying there on tables, covered from head to toe in blankets. There were doctors in there as well, eating sandwiches. Cripes, how could they do that? Just sit around and stuff their faces with dead guys lying all over the place.

Gil tried to tell himself that it was because they were there all the time. That they had simply gotten used to it. That might well be it . . . but still, he had a hard time imagining how *anyone* could ever get used to something like that.

Well . . . they had, obviously.

And they weren't just going to roll out the stiff for him.

He was just a patient, after all. If he went toddling in there and said, "Hey, lemme see ol' Matt's body," they were hardly likely to be cooperative.

This was going to take some acting.

Gil worked to make his face as slack-jawed as possible. Then he jammed his thumbs into his eyes, to make them sting so that tears would well up. The red-faced look was definitely the one to go for. He sniffed deeply a few times to add some *ooomph* to it, and then, taking a deep breath, he walked into the morgue.

He was immediately hit by the chill air that seemed to rush through. It would have to be cool, of course. Couldn't have bodies just rotting and stinking up the joint in warm air.

The two doctors looked up. They couldn't have been much older than he was. Probably first-year residents or something. Well, that made sense. If you got guys just out of med school, naturally the thing to do is start them with patients that are already dead. What's the worst that's going to happen? They can't lose the guy. He's worm food.

One of them stepped down from the table he'd been perched on and said, "Whaddayou think you're doing down here?" His surgical greens were crisp. Who was he trying to impress? The corpses?

"I . . ." Gil made sure his voice choked a moment. "I . . . a friend of mine is down here."

"Yeah, well you shouldn't be," said the other doctor.

"I wanted to say good-bye."

"Christ, you shouldn't even be out of bed." The first doctor, a tall, jowly man, had a plastic name tag that read "Barnum." The other, a taller, bearded man, was named Chase. "Look at you," said Barnum.

"I wanted to say good-bye," Gil repeated, sounding on the verge of tears. Inwardly he was congratulating himself on his performance. He was going to start choking himself up.

"What floor are you on?" demanded Chase. But he was not looking unsympathetic. "C'mon, kid. I'll bring you back upstairs . . ."

"He was my best friend!" moaned Gil. The moan wasn't difficult. It was, in fact, genuine, because his body was still protesting the amount of activity to which he was subjecting it. But he didn't care. "I'm gonna be here for a while, and I'll miss the funeral, and—and . . ."

Barnum glanced at Chase and shrugged. "Well . . . shit . . . it is Christmas Eve, after all."

Chase looked at him with a raised eyebrow. "It's Christmas Eve, and your idea of a gift is to let this kid eyeball a corpse?"

Barnum shrugged. "It's the thought that counts."

Chase signed, and a little wisp of vapor emerged from his mouth. He shivered slightly. "Christ, is it colder in here than usual?"

"I hadn't noticed."

Chase was heading toward the wall, wherein there was row upon row of heavy metal doors, like meat lockers. "What was your friend's name?"

"Olivetti," said Gil, brushing away a nonexistent tear. "Matt Olivetti."

"You mean the guys on the news?" asked Barnum. "Cripes. Sorry to hear about that, kid."

Chase was scanning the lockers, as if he could peer inside them. Then he grabbed the handle of one and pulled.

"Stuck," he muttered. "Maybe he doesn't want to come out."

He pulled harder and this time the door swung open. A fresh gust of cool air billowed out. "Christ, is the re-frigeration unit broken? What's going on here? Colder than a witch's tit." He stopped and looked at Gil. "Ever seen a stiff before, kid?"

Gil shook his head.

Matthew's body was zipped up in a plastic bag, which

suited Gil fine. Inwardly he chortled that good old Matty was ending up like a packed-up sandwich. But even as he took satisfaction in that, immediately he knew something was wrong the moment that the drawer had been pulled open.

Chase and Barnum were staring at it, too. "What the hell—?" muttered Chase.

The Velcroed bag over Matthew was opaque, so a clear view of the body wasn't possible under even the best of circumstances. But this was hardly that. The bag was covered with a thin layer of frost. Beneath that—

"What the hell is that?" said Chase, poking at the stiff bag. "Geez . . ."

Barnum pulled at the fastenings of the bag and they separated with a sound like knuckles cracking. Ice and frost broke away and clattered onto the floor. Gil was looking at the two puzzled men and was beginning to get a sinking feeling. "You guys' freezer unit break or something?"

"This isn't some goddamn freezer unit, kid," Barnum said, and then he suddenly took a step back as he managed to see inside the bag. "Jesus, look at that! Look at it! Bobby . . ."

"I see it," Chase said quickly. He was stopping Barnum immediately, because he knew that Barnum might start chattering uncontrollably over this. Better to shut him up quickly.

Gil shoved forward to try to get a better look. It didn't look any better from close up than it did from far away.

Matthew's body had been replaced by some sort of brown, encrusted . . . thing. Gil reached out and rapped on it. It felt thick and unyielding, like a coconut, and the rapping made a deep, thudding sound. And it was cold. Ice-cold.

Barnum turned to Chase. "If this is your idea of a joke—"

"Screw that," said Chase. "Get me a cutter. Hurry."

"You're gonna cut into that thing? C'mon, Bobby, that might not be smart, y'know?" said Barnum nervously. "Maybe we should call Doc Eddings—"

"Right. Right, call the senior doctor on duty, and tell him that one of our stiffs had turned into a goddamn butterfly. Jesus, Gary. Get with the program. You think Eddings is gonna wanna hear that? He already thinks we're a couple of world-class screwups after we lost that head two months ago. You wanna drag him down here and show him this? Not me, kiddo. Now get me the goddamn cutter, will ya, please?"

"Don't do it," said Gil.

Chase had virtually forgotten about him. "Get out of here, kid," he said as Barnum brought over a laser cutter. Normally it was used for slicing open a body from crotch to sternum for the purpose of performing an autopsy. It had never been used on something like this before. He hoped that it would work. Then again, part of him hoped it wouldn't.

"Okay, let's move him . . . it . . . whatever." Barnum grabbed the top end of the body bag while Chase put his arms under the lower half. They lifted, grunting, and Chase gasped out, "Thing's lighter than I thought it would be."

"Please," Gil was urging, "please, don't do it."

The two men ignored him and lay the cocoon—for want of a better term—on a table. Barnum turned and glanced at Gil. "Listen, kid," he said tiredly, "there's nothing to be scared of here, okay? We're just going to slice this open to see where the growth came from."

"It's Matthew. He's alive."

"Matthew's dead," said Chase firmly. "He came in here and his body was crushed. So don't give me this 'He's alive' bullshit, okay?" Chase was pulling on protective gloves, and he had picked up the laser cutter. "Now get the hell out of here." Without waiting to see if Gil obeyed his terse instruction, Chase turned to the job at hand.

Gil took a step back but went no farther. Chase placed the Y-shaped device against the top of the cocoon and activated it. A high-pitched whine filled the air.

"Don't do it!" said Gil, louder this time, over the sound of the cutter.

"Watch your fingers," muttered Chase to Barnum. Barnum was bracing the cocoon on the other side.

"Yeah, thanks for the tip," Barnum replied.

Chase sliced the cocoon all the way down from the top to the end, in a perfect vertical line. The frost on the outside of the cocoon did not appear to have diminished at all. It was as if it was self-regenerating.

"Spreader," said Chase.

Barnum went to the tool table and brought back the rib spreader. Chase wedged it into the opening and, with a grunt, started turning the crank. "Think they'd've gotten us a motorized one by now," he said between gritted teeth.

"Be happy we got the laser cutter," Barnum said.

Chase nodded slightly in acknowledgment. "Cheap bastards."

"They figure, why waste a lot of money. Can't collect big bills on stiffs."

"They'll find a way," Chase said. "They'll find a way to soak a body for every nickel. If this were ancient Rome, where they put coins on the eyes of the dead in order to pay their way to the afterlife—this place would remove the coins just before the bodies were carted off."

All the while as he talked, he kept turning, splitting open the cocoon wider and wider. Chill air blasted from within. Chase's fingers were getting numb. He stopped a moment and flexed them to try restoring circulation.

"Screw this," he said, and gripped one side of the fissure. "Pull," he ordered.

Barnum grasped the other side.

"Together, and—"

They yanked in opposite directions. A sound like a rifle shot exploded through the morgue.

A blast of chill steam, like dry ice, surged upward and filled the air. The temperature in the room dropped fifteen degrees in a matter of seconds and kept on going. Frost started to coat the walls.

"Close it up!" howled Gil. *"Close it up!"*

Barnum and Chase didn't hear, or if they did hear, they paid no attention. They returned to the cocoon and stared into it. All they could make out was the surging chill mist from within.

Barnum looked up at Chase. "Whaddayou think?"

"I think we call Eddings," admitted Chase. He leaned forward, trying to get a better look. "Hey, Matt?" he called jokingly, trying not to show his rapidly mounting fear. "Matty, you in there?"

A hand lashed out from within the cocoon with the speed of a cobra.

"Jesus Christ!" shrieked Barnum, leaping back.

The arm was coated with delicate eye crystals. Just beneath the surface of the skin could be seen a minuscule latticework of veins, blue and pumping blood.

The hand was wrapped around Chase's throat.

Chase gasped, his eyes bulging, and he grabbed at the arm, trying to pry it off. He tried to stammer out Barnum's name, but the pressure of the hand had closed off Chase's windpipe in the first second. In the next second, it crushed it.

Barnum staggered back, his eyes wide, his mouth moving but making no sound. Chase sagged, blood flooding his rapidly collapsing lungs. He pounded at the arm with rapidly decreasing strength.

Gil shrieked and turned, trying to run from the room. He slipped on a patch of ice and went down.

The hand shoved Chase away. Chase fell to the floor not three feet away from Gil. Gil howled again as he saw the life flee from Chase's eyes.

Matthew Olivetti sat up.

His skin was pale and delicate, and there were patches

where the new skin had developed to fill in that which had been torn. They were gently pulsing with new life. His head was at an odd angle. He looked at the hand that had just strangled Chase, and flexed the fingers, as if trying to determine whether he was pleased with it or not.

Chase's body shook once more and then stopped moving.

By that time Barnum had gotten to his feet. There was horror in his eyes but determination in his actions. He grabbed a laser scalpel and came at Matthew.

Matthew had half pulled himself from his cocoon and he glanced at Barnum with what appeared to be only passing interest. And then the chill mist in the air swirled, like a miniature hurricane, and shot toward Barnum. It enveloped him, freezing him in his tracks, entering his nostrils, his ears. He opened his mouth to scream and the mist, like a thing alive, shot down into his lungs. It froze his lungs in a matter of seconds, and the next breath he tried to take, they shattered.

Matthew was sitting up, looking tremendously rested. His cold, hard eyes narrowed as he surveyed the room, and then they rested on Gil. He extended one leg over the cocoon and then the other. He slid out of the cocoon to the floor, naked. His skin was deathly white, but his eyes seemed to be glowing with the red blaze of life. He was naked as he leaned against the table, effecting a casual pose. His fingers came to rest on the laser cutter, and he smiled, his lips drawing back in a death's-head grimace.

Gil lay on the floor, whimpering. He felt a dampness in the area of his crotch, and he managed to form some half words that made no sense.

Matthew Olivetti walked over toward him, his limbs stiff and unyielding, but loosening with every step. He crouched down next to Gil and took the terrified boy's face in his hands.

"Hello, Gil," he said softly. "It's been ages."

Gil's skin crawled as Matthew kissed him firmly on the

lips and then drew his head back. "This calls for a celebration," said Matthew. "We have to dance. But only"—and he held up the laser tool—"only if you let me cut in."

The whining of the laser cutter was barely drowned by Gil's screams that seemed to linger in the air long afterward.

18

Rommel went berserk.

The danger that had befallen Chuck bellowed in his head, a clarion call, and Rommel reared to his hind legs and started barking furiously.

The sound made the guard in the lobby of the *Tribune* building jump several feet in the air. Rommel had been stonily silent the entire time previously, so the man was totally unprepared. By the time his mind was registering that something had happened to upset the dog, Rommel was already in motion.

Rommel bolted toward a pair of elevator doors that were just in the process of closing and with a mighty leap, propelled by the powerful muscles of his hind legs, Rommel cleared the distance and landed inside the elevator car.

The three people inside screamed as Rommel landed on the carpeted interior with a resounding thud. They lunged for the Door Open button, but the elevator was already in its smooth and silent journey upward. Rommel turned his massive bulk around, barking the entire time, endeavoring to inform the moronic humans that Chuck was in trouble. Naturally they didn't understand.

"N-n-nice doggie," one of the men stammered.

Rommel glanced at him disdainfully. The dog was far more interested in the actions of the female human, who had just pressed a button on the wall that had obediently started to glow in reaction to her touch. Seconds later the elevator car stopped and the three humans ran out, screaming and shouting.

Chuck wasn't at this particular place. Rommel was sure of that . . . just as sure as he was that Chuck was somewhere above him. All he had to do was imitate the humans and sooner or later, he would find Chuck.

The humans has shown him what he had to do—when they weren't busy screaming or stammering inanities. He went up on his hind paws and slammed his forepaws along the buttons, lighting up the entire array.

One of these buttons would take him to Chuck. He was certain of it. And as soon as he was there, he was going to—

That was when a chill went through Rommel.

It wasn't related to Chuck.

Something else was happening. Something massive. Something . . .

Rommel's grasp of human concepts of morality had always been hazy at best. But this time, it cut into him like a scalpel, and he knew with complete and utter certainty.

Something evil was abroad on the land.

Chuck stopped breathing.

It was the only thing that saved him.

It hit him with the same remarkable clarity that had overwhelmed Rommel. Something had just happened. Something had been unleashed. Something of incredible psionic power, and directed only by a force of utter malevolence.

In such a circumstance, some people might have gasped and, in so doing, taken in an additional whiff of the chloroform that would have put them under completely. But in Chuck's case, everything froze. His entire respiratory system stopped, so incredible was the shock, so encompassing was the fear that shook him. His heart literally skipped a beat.

It was like a dash of cold water across his face, and although there were still some effects from the chloroform in him, his thoughts were now clear.

His next move was completely reflexive.

He twisted free in one motion, turned and grabbed Erwin's hand. He yanked the cloth away from his mouth and nose, staggering slightly, his system still fighting it off. The world tilted around Chuck and he ignored it, trying to find the calm center, and the twisted and pivoted with his hip. Erwin sailed over Chuck's head, still clutching the cloth, and landed on the far side of his desk with a crash.

The other three editors were spreading out, trying to find a clear target so they could shoot. Chuck staggered, still whoozy from the chloroform and the sudden exertion of his aikido move.

There. To his right. One of the gunmen was clear and aiming. He reached out with his mind and yanked the gun downward. It discharged harmlessly . . .

The editor screamed and went down, clutching at his foot. Blood was streaming from it. Obviously it hadn't been as harmless as all that.

Reporters were coming out of their cubicles, looking around in confusion, not understanding any of what was happening except for one thing—the hated government editors were under siege.

Erwin was hauling himself to his feet. Ignoring the yelps of the editor with the ruined foot, he shouted, "Get him! Hold him!"

Another editor came in fast, trying to bring his gun to

bear, Chuck had no time for delicacies. He caught the gun hand and kept the forearm immobile. The man's forward motion kept him going, overstraining the elbow. There was a snap and a scream. Chuck swept the man's legs out from under him and hurled him to the ground.

Incredibly, Erwin's attention was on the reporters. "Go back to your desks!" he was shouting. "This is all off the record! None of this is official!"

A barking from around the corner. Rommel was coming, and Chuck was momentarily distracted.

A gun went off just behind Chuck's ear. He felt a buzz like an angry bee streak just passt his head, and cursed himself for having lost track of his opponents. Sloppy. Sloppy and potentially deadly. He spun and there was the fourth editor, the hammer drawing back on his gun and slamming down for a second shot just as Chuck was turning. This one wasn't going to miss.

Chuck realized to his horror that his stupidity was going to cost him his life. After everything he had been through, after all the threats he had survived—blindness, the wilds of a hostile forest, the berserk rages of psionic assassins—after all that, he was going to be taken down by a simple gun by a simple government stooge.

The gun fired and Chuck lashed out with the full power of his mind just as the bullet left the gun with a roar that seemed to fill his ears.

And the bullet skidded to a halt.

In midair.

It just hung there, an impotent piece of lead.

The editor was shocked. No less so was Chuck who, never one given to profanity, nevertheless said in astonishment, "Son of a bitch."

There was a pounding on the floor like jackhammers and Rommel rounded the corner, barking furiously like a cannon fusillade. The editor saw him coming and his mouth dropped, for seeing Rommel barrel toward you was like standing at an intersection and suddenly spotting an out-of-control tractor trailer with your name on it.

He tried to bring the gun around, but it was too late as Chuck psychically pulled the gun from his hands. It sailed through the air and Chuck caught it effortlessly.

Rommel leaped, his forepaws smashing into the chest of the editor and slamming him to the ground. Rommel's massive jaws were poised over his face, ready to rip it off.

"Back off, Rommel," Chuck said tiredly. When it came to Rommel, he was starting to feel like a broken record.

Rommel glanced at him. *We going to go through this again?*

"No killing."

"Put the gun down."

That last had been Erwin's voice. Chuck turned and saw the government man, and now he was holding a gun aimed straight at Chuck. He had retreated, standing just in front of one of the multicolored thin cubicle walls. Reporters were crushing in on all sides, and he shouted again, "Get back to work! All of you!"

"We are working," said one reporter calmly.

"This is not a story! This is not sanctioned. This is not approved. This is not happening!" Erwin insisted, his gun wavering as he pointed at Chuck.

And now Chuck was aiming his own gun straight at Erwin. "Put it down," Chuck said icily. "Put it down or I'll shoot."

"No you won't," Erwin informed him. "I read your dossier. I know who you are from the fingerprints I lifted off the bottle. You won't shoot. You're opposed to violence. You hate killing. Now put the gun down. And don't try to make me point the other way, or yank the gun from my hand. If I feel the slightest motion of my body that's not my own, I'll start shooting and keep shooting. Who knows where I'll be pointing. Maybe at you. Maybe at someone else. One of these reporters gets shot, I won't give a rat's ass. But you will. You'll care. You care about a

damned thing in the world. So unless you think you can
stop a whole bunch of bullets . . ."

"No," said Chuck softly. "Probably not. I was damned
lucky to stop the one."

"Then we understand each other," said Erwin.

That's when the wall fell in on him.

The cubicle wall directly behind him suddenly crashed
forward on top of him. With a howl of pain and indig-
nation Erwin hit the floor, the gun skittering away from
him.

Lying atop Erwin—or more precisely, on top of the
wall on top of Erwin—were two bulky reporters. Chuck
understood immediately. Inside the cubicle, unseen, they
had smashed into the wall like linebackers, and had easily
sent the thing crashing down on top of the hapless Erwin.

Erwin, for his part, didn't understand anything except
that he was being crushed. "What's happening?!" he
screamed. "Simon! This is your doing. I warned you—"

"Yes, you did," said Chuck calmly. "You didn't warn
them, though," and he inclined his head slightly toward
the reporters atop him.

"Oh, he warned us," said the bulkier of the two. "He
warned us that he didn't give a rat's ass if we were shot
by stray bullets."

"You wouldn't have been shot," Chuck informed them
with just a trace of smugness. "While he was yammering,
I took control of the gun's trigger. It wouldn't have moved
if he'd yanked on it from now to doomsday."

The was when the building shook.

The sensation made Chuck's earlier experience with
earthquakes seem like a child's game. Everything, everything was shaking, and there was a roar like crashing
waves. All around him, people—hardened reporters, veteran earthquake survivors—people were screaming.

The force was tremendous. Desks were overturned. The
glass in the wall cubicles shattered. Anything that was on

a desk was hurled to the floor, and all around Chuck was the sound of falling hardware.

The building actually tilted, sending Chuck off his feet. Automatically he shoved the gun in his pocket, afraid that if he hurled it somewhere it might go off upon landing, or worse, one of those moronic government editors might get their hands on it. He tumbled back and then slammed into something furry and hard.

"Rommel!" he shouted.

Get off me!

Overhead lighting fixtures shattered and fell to the ground, smashing all around them. Chuck saw one start to plummet toward the unprotected head of a reporter and his mind knocked it aside, making it drop a foot to the right of the man.

The wall cubicles collapsed, shaken apart from their fastenings by the violence of the quake. Like a massive set of dominoes, they fell, one atop the other, knocking everything apart. People were shouting to get out of the way or were pinned under them, putting all their strength against them to shove them aside.

Moments later it stopped, just as suddenly as it started.

Of everyone in the city room, only Chuck and Rommel knew what had just happened, and of those two, only Chuck fully understood. He had sensed the pulsing fury behind the quake. He knew that it was unnatural.

"Get me out of here! Get me out!" Erwin was screaming.

"Fuck you," said the city editor, savoring each word, as if he had been storing it up for ages, looking for the proper moment. He turned to Chuck. "You're a major story. That stuff you were doing—a weapon of some kind?"

"Of some kind," Chuck admitted. "I think you're going to have a more major story than me in a minute or two, though."

"That was a hell of a quake," said the city editor. "I've

been through some beauties, and that was—"

"The first," said Chuck. "Only the first. And only the beginning. Look." And he pointed.

The city editor looked where Chuck was pointing, toward a window.

Snow was falling, thick and fast and savage.

A blizzard.

The city editor turned back toward Chuck, trying to find words and none coming—a curious situation for a reporter to be in.

"What I said about doomsday," Chuck admitted, "may have been ill-timed. I need to find Carmen Friedman."

"She's not in," said the editor distractedly. He was staring at the snow, ignoring the moans from the injured government editors all around him.

"I need to find her. Tell me where she lives."

"That's confidential. Jenkins! Get the weather bureau on the phone! Find out—"

"Dammit!" shouted Chuck, and he grabbed the man by the shoulders and whirled him around. "You don't understand! I've got to find her, and right now! Or there's going to be more earthquakes!"

"Don't be absurd," said the city editor incredulously. "Carmen's causing the earthquakes? Is that what you're saying?"

"You're not dealing with earthquakes. You're dealing with a an angry, demented teenager, and Carmen Friedman knows more about him than anyone, and she's more than she seems. Now tell me where she is! Her phone number is unlisted, and I'd rather deal with you than the phone company. Tell me!"

"You're nuts! You're fucking nuts! Get away from me!"

Chuck had had it. There was no time for subtlety. "Rommel, tear his legs off."

"I'll get my Rolodex," said the city editor.

19

Matthew Olivetti stepped out into his world.

It was Christmas Eve, rapidly approaching Christmas Day. The day that many believed to be the day that earth's savior was born.

Matthew stood at the top of Telegraph Hill and laughed low in his throat. "Where is your savior now?" he said.

The blizzard swirled around him, and he didn't feel the bite of the chill air at all. He was wearing clothes taken from the men, and the teenager, who lay dead back in the hospital morgue. His hair was standing on end, his body crackling with power.

He had changed. Metamorphosized. He had become something better, something unique, something very, very special.

He started down Telegraph Hill. Every step sent seismic shockwaves through the ground. Buildings, supposedly earthquake-proof, toppled. Around him, all around him were screams and shouts and howls of "This is it! This is the Big One!"

The Big One. The earthquake that would send California into the ocean, for once and for all. No more concerns.
No more pussyfooting around. Just hundreds of miles of
oceanfront property.

The whole state? Could he sink the whole state?

He felt he could.

State, hell. The country. He could sense the fault lines
throughout the continent. He could split them wide, sending the entire country spilling down into the bowels of
the earth.

The whole country? Hell, the whole world.

Far, far beneath his feet, he drew a sense of the molten
core. He felt power roiling in him, the ability to draw that
magma upward, oozing and blasting through every avail-
able crevice. Everywhere, the earth would bleed lava. He
could make the world crack apart. Every man, woman,
and child, every animal, every tree . . . all his. His for the
taking.

He stretched out a hand, imagining them all sitting in
his palm, trembling and quivering with fear. As well they
should. As well they goddamn should.

He closed his fist. Two blocks away, an apartment
building dropped into a massive sinkhole that hadn't been
there the previous day. Twenty-seven people died within
seconds.

It wasn't enough. Not nearly enough.

His eyes blazed as they swept the city. His city. Snow
was coating the ground, two inches deep and spinning
about like a whirlpool. More snow was falling, large,
white flakes upon his face. He looked skyward, welcom-
ing it. Like a child, he stuck out his tongue, collecting
flakes on it.

They melted on his tongue, and he realized they made
his mouth feel dirty. "Pollution," he muttered. "Filth . . ."

Filth. The filth who had murdered his parents. The filth
who did not deserve to live.

Somewhere in this great city of filth was the murderer.

The Psi-Man. He was behind it. Matthew's eyes narrowed as an image of the only other psionic he'd ever met—that Psi-Man—danced in his mind.

His enemy. He must have been in on it with the woman. He must have told the woman who had bombed them what to do. Chuck—good old Chuck—like Matthew, was one of the superior beings. The beings destined to rule. So he must have told the woman to plant that bomb. She must have been under his orders. It only made sense. A superior being would never have an underling acting in such a manner without his knowledge. He must have known, so he must have approved. That simple. That easy.

Matthew reached out, trying to get a sense of Chuck.

He wasn't absolutely sure yet, but he trusted the instincts that guided him. He started across town, every step leaving seismic shocks in his wake. The heart of the storm followed him, fearsome and biting. Any lesser being caught unprotected in the traveling snowstorm would lose limbs to frostbite within minutes.

Chuck and the woman—Friedman, her name had been—they were going to lose a lot more than limbs.

Emergency vehicles, unprepared for the insane weather, skidded and became mired in snowdrifts that had literally sprung from nowhere. A couple of cops were trying to shove their car out of its entrapment in one such drift when Matthew stalked past. He was easy to spot. The ground was rumbling beneath each step. If they had looked very closely, they would have realized that he was actually walking about an inch above the surface.

They did not notice that, but the older of the tow cops was enough of a veteran to realize that something was wrong.

He turned toward Matthew, pulling his heavy-duty service weapon, an RBG-PD. He gripped the large gun with both hands, which were already becoming stiff and unyielding since he had no gloves, and shouted, "Hold it! You! *Hold it!*"

Matthew turned toward him slowly, as if a gnat had just drawn itself to his attention.

When Matthew spoke, it was with a sepulchral, sonorous tone like the striking of a gong signaling Armageddon.

"Don't you mean . . . freeze?" he asked.

The cop never had a chance to move as the snow hit him. The winds howled to gale force about him and his body disappeared within, a cone of ice and snow enveloping him. His fingers tightened reflexively from the freezing air, and a bullet passed harmlessly a good three feet from Matthew. He smiled and watched with fascination as, within seconds, the cop was transformed into a human snowman. The fierce storm around the police officer subsided, and all that was left was a man encased in rock-hard ice. He was in the same position as before, gun extended, a living statue.

The other, younger cop reacted immediately. He leaped into the car and grabbed the radio. He started screaming for help, the codes for officers in distress and officers down completely forgotten. He just began howling for someone, anyone to help them.

Matthew watched him for a long moment, and the cop sensed that he was under that inhuman gaze. The Chaos Kid contemplated him for what seemed an eternity and then said complacently, "You're not worth it," and turned away.

The young cop, whose wife was expecting next month, and who had been briefly sure that he was never going to see his baby, let out a long, unsteady breath.

Matthew turned back.

"Screw it," he said, and stomped his foot once on the ground.

A fissure blossomed forth from beneath his foot, rippling out and under the police car. The car slid into it and the cop's scream was cut off by the sound of the earth slamming back together again. By that time Matthew was already two blocks away and heading toward where his instincts guided him.

Toward his prey.

20

Carmen Friedman had stopped looking out the window of her apartment in the Marina district. The steady falling snow was unnerving enough; she didn't have to keep subjecting herself to it.

Every so often the floor of her apartment would shake. It had been a faint tremor first, but they had become progressively stronger. It was as if a giant were approaching, taking mammoth steps, and the world was vibrating beneath each huge footfall. It was a mental image that was somewhat disturbing.

She had decided that a vacation was in order.

Once it was discovered what she had done, she knew her life would be worthless. But she had acted as she felt she had to. She had taken a course of action, driven by conscience and a protective instinct for the safety of humanity. It sounded grandiose, but she believed in it. She also believed in self-preservation, and was rapidly packing almost everything she owned for the purpose of preserving herself.

There was a brisk knock at her door.

She wasn't expecting anyone.

She didn't want anyone.

There might be a harmless salesman on the other side of the door. Or there might not be.

She was not a woman prone to taking needless risk. She pulled a gun from her handbag, brought it up firmly, braced with both hands, and started firing. Huge wood chips flew from the door as the bullets penetrated, slamming through and unquestionably perforating the individual on the other side. Part of her prayed that it had not been an innocent person knocking at her door. Another part of her didn't care whether her prayer was answered or not.

She didn't stop until she had emptied the entire clip. She ejected it and started to pull another clip from her handbag.

The door suddenly flew open as if propelled by a gale wind, and Chuck Simon walked in and stretched out his hand. Carmen gasped as the clip and the gun sailed across the room and into his hand.

Rommel was right behind Chuck, growling, his tail straight out and back as if ready to pounce. Chuck calmly slammed the clip home and aimed the gun at Carmen. "Why did you do it?" His voice was like ice.

She raised an eyebrow and half smiled. "You won't shoot me," she said. "Killing is anathema to you."

A single gunshot sounded in the apartment as the lamp to Carmen's immediate right exploded. Carmen never wavered, never so much as reacted. "Missed," she said.

"Just as you did when you tried to shoot me through the door," Chuck told her. "Unfortunately for you, I've got a sort of sixth sense about such things. What if it had been your neighbors?"

"I was planning to move, so they wouldn't be my neighbors in any event," she said calmly. "Besides, I happen to know they're out of town on vacation. Enjoying the holidays in New York." She laughed once. "They said they miss snow. Just think of all the money they could have saved."

"This is his doing."

She nodded slowly. "Yes, I figured that."

"We've got to stop him."

" 'We,' Paleface?"

"Yes, we.

"Screw that. I'm leaving."

She reached for her handbag and there was another shot, to her left, taking a huge chunk out of a coffee table and sending it spinning back. She turned on him, her face twisted in fury, her hands balled into fists. "Dammit!" she shouted. "Stop screwing around! I know you won't shoot me. I know about your precious philosophies. I know about the men you've killed in the past, and how you've sworn never to kill again. I know your goddamn IQ and shoe size! I know everything about you, so stop playing these macho asshole games and pretending that you're going to blow me away!"

He stared at her for a long moment. Then he ejected the ammo clip from the gun and tossed the useless weapon back to her.

"Who in hell are you?" he asked.

The ground suddenly rumbled beneath them. They staggered, grabbing at whatever was nearby to maintain their balance. She held on to the edge of a couch, he on to the frame of the nearest door. They held their breath until, long seconds later, it had stopped.

"Who are you?" he repeated. "You blew up the Olivetti house. You did it with ruthless efficiency. You knew exactly what you were going to do before you did it."

"Of course I did. What, you think I'm in the habit of carrying a bomb in my purse?" she said dryly.

"*I* don't know! Maybe you are!" he said in exasperation, waving his arms in the air. "I thought I knew you or understood you. I thought you were a dedicated reporter, but that's all. Now I find out you carry bombs in your purse. For all I know, you've got a cruise missile stashed in your bra."

She looked down speculatively, a bemused eyebrow cocked. "Flatterer," she said.

Rommel growled next to him. *He's coming. I can feel it.*

"So can I," said Chuck.

You going to let me chew on her? You told me to chew on the other one, the man, and then you stopped me. That wasn't nice. You shouldn't get my hopes up like that.

"It may come to that."

"You're talking with the dog, right?" she said. "I just didn't want to think I was missing anything."

He crossed the room and grabbed her wrist firmly. "I'm missing something," he said tightly. "I'm missing the main reason for all of this. Now tell me, blast it! I'm entitled to know!"

She sighed. "All right. I suppose it doesn't matter anymore. I'm a spy. A Russian spy."

"You'll have to do better than that."

"I am!" she said. "Really!"

He sensed that she was telling the truth, and yet, it was absurd. "You are not. Russian? That's ridiculous. That's—"

Carmen proceeded to speak in flawless Russian, complete with an extremely authentic accent. Chuck's eyes widened as she stopped speaking and stared at him defiantly with flashing eyes.

"What did you just say?" he asked, feeling inane.

"I said you were hurting my wrist and could you please let go."

"Oh." He did so and stepped away, studying her speculatively. "A Russian spy."

"I'd think someone who spent time with the Complex would not be so impressed by meeting yet another spy."

"So I assume your name isn't Carmen Friedman."

"I'll tell you everything if you'll just get us the hell out of here."

He nodded. "Yeah. Yeah, okay. Let's go."

No chewing on her?

"No chewing on her."

They hurried outside after Carmen hurriedly grabbed up her valise and a couple of other personal belongings. Sitting outside, coated with snow, windshield wipers moving furiously, was the RAC. They all climbed in, the snow billowing around them. Chuck yanked the door shut and gunned the engine.

He turned onto Lombard Street, Route 101, and started heading west. "Russian spy," he said again, shaking his head. "That's so bizarre. A Russian spy living at the Marina."

"Yes, well, I couldn't get an apartment in Russian Hill," she said sarcastically. "What are you going to do with me?"

"Frankly, I don't know."

"I assumed you were going to sacrifice me to the boy terror."

"It had crossed my mind," he admitted. "But now I'm not quite sure how I can do that. I still don't understand how you could've done what you did, Carm—what is your name, anyway?"

"Alexandra Romanova," she said. "My friends and co-workers call me Alex."

"Alex," he said. "Boy's name."

"You always know just what to say. If it's of any consolation, the suffix 'ova' means 'daughter of.' Happy?"

"Ecstatic."

He stayed on Route 101 as it angled off right onto Richardson. He saw signs for the Golden Gate Bridge. Sounded as good as anyplace.

"And how did a Russian spy get involved with a priest?" he asked.

"He wasn't a priest. He was a fellow operative, named Nikko."

He stared at her. "What?" His voice was barely above a whisper.

"Nikko was my partner," she said.

"Are you saying," he asked slowly and carefully, "that I was set up? Again? *Again?*"

"Your presence in San Francisco was brought to my attention by my superior," she said, adding a distinctly Russian accent to the last word. "I was ordered to subtly enlist your aid in the capture of Matthew Olivetti, the most formidable and powerful psionic individual that anyone has been able to detect. Nikko's cover identity was a priest, just as mine was a reporter. We didn't just step off the boat, my friend. We've been here for quite some time. It took both Nikko and myself months to set up these identities. I'm not especially happy to have to give mine up."

He slammed a fist onto the wheel.

"Charles, please hold your temper," Rac said briskly.

He ignored the car's annoyed tone. All around him, cars were mired in snow. He felt the powerful engine of Rac laboring to keep them moving smoothly on 101. The wind howled outside the windows. Thermal installations throughout the windows were managing to just barely keep up with melting the snow that was endeavoring to collect on them. He was staking his life on his car. Maybe he should reconsider his attitude. "Sorry," he muttered.

Did you just apologize to the—

"Quiet, Rommel."

Alex reflexively glanced back at the dog, who looked utterly silent to her. He seemed to be glaring at her.

"So let me get this straight," he said. "You and your Russian pal got together and decided to scam me. And I fell for it."

"We chose scenarios from old American films," she said. "We thought it would make an acceptable story upon which to hinge your belief. A priest, after all, would be more likely to be conversant with the spawn of Satan than he would psionics. And your own innate faith enabled you to accept Nikko's divine inspiration to turn to you."

"You people stink, you know that? The Complex pulled the same crap on me, ages ago. Played me for a fool. You'd think I'd've learned by now. You'd think—"

"You are so stinking self-centered!" she shouted. "You think you're the only one with problems?" Rommel growled warningly in the rear, and she became dimly aware that her back was exposed to the gaping jaws of the massive canine. If he took exception to her tone of voice, she could wind up a doggie treat very quickly.

But she pressed on. "Nikko lost his life! Matthew Olivetti killed him! Nothing is going to change that. You want more? I not only have the psionic monster on my tail— how, I don't know, but this weather, the earthquakes, it's got to be him—not only is he after me, but I disobeyed direct orders from my boss. I was told to recruit Olivetti. Enlist him. Bring that human nuclear weapon over to our side. I, on my own, decided otherwise. I decided he was too dangerous to live, after what he did to Nikko. After I realized what else he was capable of. I took things into my own hands and determined that I would eliminate him. Do you understand the significance of that?"

He had a feeling he did. "Your bosses won't be happy."

"My bosses will be terminally unhappy, and I will be the terminal individual," she said. "I acted from my conscience, out of what I felt was going to be for the good of humanity. So don't complain to me about feeling used, Chuck. Nikko gave up his life, and the chances are extremely good that I have also. I have enough problems without your hurt feelings."

"Yeah, but you botched it, didn't you. Matthew is still alive, and causing—"

And suddenly 101 wrenched wildly beneath them.

Chuck completely lost control of the wheel, but Rac

did not. Lights flickered across the display panel. Rac sped up.

Chuck's head slammed against the window. From the back seat, Rommel barked in protest.

"Seismic disturbance," Rac tonelessly informed them.

He grabbed at the wheel and immediately felt that he wasn't controlling the car anymore. "Give me back the steering!" he shouted.

"Not advisable."

"Do it!"

"Not advisable."

All around them, cars were skidding, smashing into concrete median strips. Considerable work had been done on the 101, since it was the main artery into the Golden Gate. That work was now in the process of being totally trashed.

"Blast it. Rac, give me back the steering! I will be in control of my own life!"

"So will I, Charles," said Rac briskly. The car started a small skid, but Rac quickly compensated, turning with it and then using the force to its own advantage. Barely an instant later the vehicle was speeding up again, grace-fully maneuvering around stalled or cracked-up cars. "Look around you. All the other cars are being controlled by humans. Their reflexes—and yours—can't match mine. That is because I don't have reflexes. I have micro-chips. I anticipate all possible trajectories and appropriate responses, at all times, within a billionth of a second, while simultaneously conducting a conversation with you. Would you like to hear some music?"

Chuck sat back, his head starting to hurt. "You're really getting on my nerves, you know that?"

"We are being pursued by an individual who can, judg-ing by his current direction and activities, be presumed to be hostile."

He craned his neck, as did Rommel, as did Carmen or Alex or whatever the hell her name was.

Half a mile behind them, closing fast, was a miniature white cyclone.

Incredibly, in the hideous weather, in the snow and ice, in the traffic-congested, earth-rocking road that they were on, Rac picked up speed. It wasn't exactly road rally velocity, but it was fast.

Perhaps not fast enough. Definitely not fast enough.

And in the middle of that cyclone, suspended, was a small, dark form. The winds and ice were carrying him high, caressing him as if he were a child spawned of the very elements. Which was, to all intents in purposes, apparently the case.

Chuck's eyes narrowed. "It's him."

Hers narrowed as well. "You're kidding."

He turned to her. "Do I look like I'm kidding?"

"No. You look like you're scared shitless."

"That's because I feel him, up here," and he tapped his head. "I'm sensing his power. I feel like my head's going to explode, just from sympathetic vibrations."

"Well, I'm not feeling too sympathetic right now, thanks," she said.

Looming up now in front of them, not too far in the distance, was the Golden Gate Bridge. It towered high, a colossus forged by man. A symbol of a time when the ingenuity of Americans was devoted to creating rather than tearing down, of bringing things to light rather than hiding in darkness.

At the moment its spires were becoming coated with ice and snow. Even from where they were, even with the snow swirling about them, they could see that traffic had slowed to a crawl.

The ground rumbled ominously beneath them.

"I have to stop him," said Chuck.

She took a breath. "You," she told him, "are out of your fucking mind."

"I have to reason with him. Make him see—"

"*Reason* with him?!"

"Yes."

"You can't reason with that!" and she pointed behind them. The swirl was growing closer. "You can't bargain with that! You can only run from that!"

"Rac, we can't go this way," Chuck said urgently. "There's too many traffic, too many people around."

"There is no other exit off this road, Charles," Rac promptly informed him. "We have to access the Golden Gate Bridge."

"Then stop."

"Unable to comply," Rac told him. "If I do, we will fall into the crevice."

"*What* crevice?" he demanded. The ground was rumbling beneath them again, louder than before. He grabbed for some sort of support.

"The one pursuing us."

He looked back again. The ground was splitting open behind them, as if a demonic mole were on their tail, breaking the earth apart to get to them.

"Keep going," Chuck said.

Just ahead was the bridge. There was a toll booth ahead. It was fully automated; drivers were supposed to insert their Cards.

"Go through," said Chuck with the funny feeling that Rac would have done so anyway.

The crevice stopped several yards behind them as Rac hurtled forward and slammed through the wooden barrier arm, sending shards flying.

We're going to die.

"Maybe," Chuck informed Rommel tersely, and then amended, "probably."

No more food.

"No."

That sucks:

"You're right."

Rac skidded to a halt. Cars were a tangled mass of immobile metal. Vehicles had skidded, smashing into barriers and other cars. People were honking their horns and screaming, the earth was rumbling with a doomsday noise, and everywhere, everywhere was the hideous howling of the wind.

Chuck shoved open the car door. "I'm going."

Alex looked at him incredulously. "Where?"

"Anywhere. Forward. Don't you understand? He's homing in on me. He senses me. And he figures you're with me."

"Lucky guess."

"So if I keep moving, that gives you a chance. So unless you've got any last-minute advice you can give me . . ."

"Talking to him won't help."

"Besides that."

Her eyes were cold. "Kill him if you can."

"If I kill him, I've lost," said Chuck.

"He's a murderer. He's berserk. You can't reason with a natural disaster. Your beliefs are wonderful. I think they're great. If things were more relaxed, I'd probably consider them a turn-on. But not now. Do something. Do anything. But stop him."

"The beliefs that you think have no place here," he told her, "are keeping you alive. You killed two innocent people, remember? His parents. You're what set him off. And I'm risking my life to save you."

"He would have gone off sooner or later. I didn't want this. You know that."

He said nothing, but got out of the car. Rommel came after him. "Stay, Rommel."

Not this time.

Chuck was about to argue, but didn't. He stepped aside as Rommel's massive body insinuated itself out of the car.

Alex Romanova said, "Hey, Chuck."

He stopped and looked back at her. "Yeah?"

"You sure know how to show a girl an exciting Christmas. I'll keep New Year's Eve open for you."

The chill wind was cutting through him. Much closer now was the whirling whiteness that was holding Matt Olivetti aloft.

"You do that," he said, and ran.

21

Chuck dodged between the unmoving cars, bumping into other people who had the same idea. He glanced over his shoulder, his mind warning him of what his eyes were already telling him. Matthew was right behind him, coming up fast and propelled by wings of wind.

Rommel stayed right behind Chuck as best he could. Snow was coating his fur, and unlike Chuck, he couldn't raise an arm to try to block off the swirling white stuff. He lowered his head. *Do something.*

"I'm working on it."

He needed to draw Matthew as far from Carmen as he could. With the aid of a slight psionic push, he jumped up onto the nearest car roof. He glanced right and left and then started running across the tops of the unmoving cars. Drivers of the cars yelled in furious protest, but they were quickly silenced when Rommel's imposing form followed Chuck a moment later.

He jumped from one car to the next, and the next. People were pushing and shoving all around, trying to find someplace to go. In the distance were the sounds of police sirens—they were probably coming to close the bridge off.

Far below, the waters of the bay were surging with incredible ferocity. Huge waves lapped up, roaring over the piers at the bottom of the tower legs.

Chuck skidded on one of the roofs and tumbled onto the snow-covered asphalt. He ran to the edge of the bridge and leaned over the railing, looking down.

The tower legs were beginning to shake, the very ground in which the bridge was anchored shifting dangerously.

Could Matthew collapse the entire bridge? Probably. Would he? Why not? Nothing had seemed to deter him thus far.

Matthew was coming in fast, riding the winds.

Tiring of climbing across cars, Rommel had dropped down and gone in between, employing the simple expedient of barking furiously at any humans in his way. It proved terribly effective.

Chuck climbed atop a railing, crouching against the gale force that surrounded him.

What now? Rommel asked.

"We have to get his attention," Chuck said. The winds were screaming so loudly that he couldn't hear his own voice, but he knew that Rommel could since the words formed inside the dog's head.

The dark figure in the midst of the cyclone was now a few hundred yards away.

"Stay here," said Chuck.

He took a deep breath, fighting his vertigo. He'd always had some problems with heights, and this was one hell of a height. He knew what he wanted to do, but his legs were paralyzed, refusing to obey the directions of his mind. He took a deep breath, glanced in the direction of Matthew's personal conveyance from hell, and then pushed off with his legs.

He leaped off the bridge.

He felt a howl of alarm from Rommel inside his head and then he started to spiral downward toward the lapping waters of the bay.

The world spun dizzingly beneath him, the waves lapping up toward him. The time that he was in midair seemed to stretch for an eternity.

It was, in fact, barely seconds. The wind snared him, lifting him up with the same sort of gentleness that it was obviously supporting Matthew. Chuck rose into the air, and people saw him and pointed, screaming, but their screams were lost in the near-gale-force winds that surrounded them.

Chuck kept going, up, up, and suddenly the wind cut out from under him. He dropped, but only a couple of feet, as he landed on a massive main cable, one of the long cables that ran between the huge towers.

He crouched down, clinging on. He had to be a hundred feet up, and far below him was the water.

From his viewpoint now, he saw the Marina in flames. Gas lines must have exploded somewhere, or perhaps gasoline tanks had been ruptured. The rumbling was increasing, the bridge shaking, and if it hadn't been for his TK, he would have been hurled from the cable. As it was, even with the power of his mind, he could barely hold on.

Matthew Olivetti landed on the cable five feet in front of him.

Whereas Chuck was on his hands and knees, holding on desperately, Matthew stood there with utter nonchalance. He smiled lopsidedly—actually smiled. His skin was pale, like a vampire, as if the blood were gone from him. His hair was wild, his eyes blazing. He was barely recognizable as the calm, collected teenager that Chuck had met barely days before.

Matthew said something and Chuck didn't even come close to hearing it. The rumble of the earth and the shrieking of the wind completely drowned out any hope of communication. Chuck screamed so loudly that he thought he'd injured a vocal cord as he cried out, *"Could you turn the volume down please!!"*

Matthew tilted his head slightly, as if not understanding the request. Then his face lit up, and almost immediately the howling of the gale subsided just enough for words to be heard, if shouted.

"Merry Christmas," said Matthew.

Chuck nodded slightly.

"That was very foolish. That jump of yours," Matthew said. "You didn't know for sure that I would save you."

"Yes, I did. You want me because you blame me for your parents' death."

"I've been thinking about it," Matthew said. He sounded as calm as if they were tossing back hot chocolates in a ski lodge. "I had thought at first—after my re-awakening—that you were responsible. Now, though, I've decided that the woman acted on her own. I don't think you have the guts for cold-blooded murder."

"Thanks."

"Where is she?"

"I don't know."

"Ah, now you see," and Matthew raised a scolding finger. "You're covering for her. You're making me think you approved of what she did. If you support that—"

"I don't think what she did was right," Chuck said. "I don't believe in killing. I hate killing."

"She wanted to kill me," Matthew said thoughtfully. "She almost did, you know. The earth saved me. The earth showed me how to survive, how to mend. I could never have gotten out of my healing cocoon unless the doctors had cut me out, but fate arranged for that. Fate is helping the earth to help me. The earth needs me."

"Why?" shouted Chuck, for the winds were starting to come up stronger. "Why does the earth need you!"

"Because the earth wants to kill itself," Matthew told him, a demented gleam in his eyes. "All the pollution that's been inflicted on it. It's too much. The earth is suffering, struggling in its death agony. Can't you feel it? Can't you sense it, everywhere you go?" His voice was starting to quiver. "I can. *I* can feel it. It hurts, like a hot rock in my stomach. It wants me to put it out of its misery. And I will." He drew himself up, brushing away the beginnings of a tear. "But I have to take care of business first. Where's the woman? Tell me."

"Can't do that."

"You idiot!" shouted Matthew.

The bay, impossibly, sent waves hurling upward that were over two hundred feet high.

"You see that!" Matthew said. "I could flood this whole bridge! I could sink this whole bridge! I could kill you with a snap of my fingers!"

"But you won't," said Chuck, "because you want her, and you figure I'm the only one who could bring you to her."

Matthew stormed down the cable and grabbed Chuck by the front of his jacket. "Don't fuck with me!" screamed the teenager.

Chuck brought his arms up with blinding speed, speed aided by desperation. He swept one arm up and the other he grabbed by the wrist. A quick twist and pivot, miraculously keeping his balance on the cable, and Chuck suddenly had Matthew's arm twisted around behind his back. The boy was doubled over, gasping.

"I could break your arm!" shouted Chuck. "I could break your neck! I could kill you!"

"Don't flatter yourself," Matthew told him. He struggled in Chuck's grip and shrieked, because all he was doing was putting more pressure on his own arm.

"I want to help you!" said Chuck. "You have incredible power, and incredible anger. You're like every teenager. You have an attitude—but in your case, you have the power to back it up. Let me help you understand that power! Let me teach you how to live with it. I know what power can do to you. No one knows it better than I do. I almost went crazy from my power, and it's only a fraction of yours. I can imagine what it's done to you. I can put myself in your place, understand you as no one else can. Come with me! We'll leave San Francisco, get out of here. We'll—"

Matthew slowly turned toward him. "You'd really do all that for me?"

"Yes," said Chuck.

Matthew actually smiled, and then he said, "You are so full of shit it's incredible."

A blast of snow smashed into Chuck's face, startling him, and he lost his grip on Matthew. The boy twisted away, laughing hysterically. Chuck went down to his knees. He was losing all feeling in his fingers from the arctic wind and snow.

Chuck tried to get up and Matthew aimed a kick at his face. Chuck saw it coming and deflected it with his mind. Matthew stumbled but then quickly recovered. He stood there, shaking his head.

Had Chuck meant all that? He wasn't sure himself. Matthew was responsible for a disaster that had killed hundreds, maybe thousands. He had to be brought to accounting for that. At the same time, who could hold him accountable? Who could possibly enforce it? He couldn't be arrested, brought to trial. With his power, he didn't have to put up with it, and wouldn't. Could he be allowed to just walk away from it? And what would he learn from that? That he could do what he wanted, when he wanted, heedless of the consequences. What a wonderful lesson for a teenager to learn.

He had to be dealt with. He had to be judged. He had to be punished.

And Chuck was the only one around who could do it, the only one vaguely capable. He didn't ask for it. He didn't want it. But it had fallen to him.

"Matthew," said Chuck, feeling a hundred years older, "it's over. It's over."

"Hell no, Chuck," Matthew replied. "It's just beginning. In a few hours, I'll be eighteen years old. I'll be legal. That means I'll be an adult. Deciding to end the world—that's an adult decision. Just as it was adults who decided to turn it into a floating pile of garbage in the first place."

Chuck couldn't argue with that, just as he couldn't afford to knock the self-imposed restraint that Matthew seemed to have put on himself. He'd fixated on his eighteenth birthday as when he would come into his full power. There was a better-than-even chance that Matthew was already capable of what he intended to do. But he'd told himself he had to wait, and convinced himself. It was the only thing Chuck had going for him.

And then Matthew's eyes widened.

"Hey. I just realized . . . on the East Coast . . . I'm eighteen already."

Chuck lashed out with his full psionic power.

Matthew sensed it coming and the winds yanked him upward, like a puppet on a string. Chuck's TK blast sailed past him and hit the cable, sending a jolt along its length.

Matthew hovered over him. "Not nice, Chuck," he scolded. "I can detect any time you try to use your ability. Just as you can when I do. But you can't dodge mine."

Chuck felt the air in his lungs start to frost. He gagged, unable to breathe.

"Where is she, Chuck," said Matthew. "Last chance to buy an extra minute for earth." Even as he spoke he was reaching downward, probing the substrata, caressing the magma core miles beneath.

There was a roar, followed by a female shout.

Both of the psionics looked down. There, on the cable, climbing toward them, was Alexandra Romanova. Directly behind her was Rommel.

"Stay away from her!" shouted Chuck, but Matthew

was already wafting toward her. He was smiling. His hand was outstretched toward her.

She had her gun out, her face set, and she aimed at Matthew.

Gun.

A gun.

"Oh, my God," said Chuck, and grabbed at his jacket pocket.

Matthew floated over Alex and chortled, "I'll get you, my pretty, and your mangy little dog, too." And he cackled, delighted with his own joke.

The air around Alex and Rommel crystallized. Alex gasped, and she squeezed the trigger reflexively.

It clicked harmlessly. Chuck had removed the ammo clip.

Do something! howled Rommel, his fur icing over. Chuck made no response.

"Chuck!" screamed Alex, or tried to, as her lungs filled with cold air and her blood started to freeze.

Matthew laughed, the sounds of the rumbling growing louder, the sky swirling overhead, and the ocean roaring beneath, all bowing, all praising their savior.

And Matthew's shoulder exploded.

He spun in midair, gasping, shocked.

Chuck was crouching on the cable, holding the gun that he'd taken away from the government editor.

Tears were streaming down Chuck's face as he fired again and again.

Matthew's body jerked about as some bullets missed but more found their mark. The look on his face was of utter astonishment.

The trigger clicked. Chuck was out of ammo.

Matthew was hovering, but erratically, still trying to recover. He was losing blood fast. Then he started to sink.

Alex was gasping for breath. Matthew's attack momentarily stilled.

And suddenly Matthew zoomed in, with one sudden

burst of speed, and slammed into Alex. With a scream, Alex lost her grip on the cable and tumbled off.

Chuck desperately reached out and grabbed Alex with his power, holding her in midair.

"Her or him!" shouted Matthew, drawing strength from who-knew-where, and turned his sights on Rommel.

Rommel seemed frozen, immobile, and then suddenly the great dog lunged forward and clamped his teeth on to Matthew's leg. Matthew tried to pull away, and kicked at the animal's face with his other leg. Rommel didn't even have enough strength to project a thought to Chuck, but he hung on with determination.

"I'll kill you, *you fucker!*" howled Matthew.

And Chuck leaped, kicking off against the cable with his psi power in order to gain an extra push.

Alex screamed as she started to fall and then Chuck devoted a portion of his mind back to her even as he slammed into Matthew.

The two of them struggled in midair. Chuck's mind was everywhere—on Alex, easing her to the ground, on Rommel . . . and on the kid who was out to kill him.

He started to feel warm.

His blood began to boil, his beard crisping.

Matthew smiled dementedly as he turned up the heat.

Images of Chuck's nightmare came to him. Frying, burning, burning alive, forever, forever in agony and pain and—

Chuck blew out Matthew's chest.

The Chaos Kid spun back, clawing at the air, but still clutching on to Chuck's hair with one hand. Chuck couldn't shove him away. His limbs were exhausted, paralyzed. He had nothing left. He was covered with Matthew's blood.

They spiraled down toward the water, Matthew clutching him close. For one moment Chuck saw there the scared expression of an eighteen-year-old kid.

And then a wave slammed into them, separating them.

Chuck went under, the world turning cold and black around him, surging and violent.

He pinwheeled his arms, determined not to panic. Around him the water was churning, but the howling had stopped. The sounds had changed, and he was sure he could hear a scream echoing through the inky darkness.

He lost track of up and down. But he let out a few air bubbles and watched which way they went, and then swam after them.

He felt the air pounding against his lungs, stinging him. His brain desperately wanted him to inhale, regardless of the fact that he was surrounded by water. He tried to ignore the pounding, the pain that seemed overwhelming.

And then he broke surface. He gasped in lungfuls of air gratefully, and then he started to swim toward a pier at the bottom of a tower leg.

The water was already subsiding as he pulled himself up onto the concrete platform. The snow had stopped as suddenly as it had begun, the gale-force winds easing into a gentle breeze.

He sat there for what seemed a long time, just staring, staring into the darkened water. Lights from the bridge overhead played against the surface of the bay.

And then he started to sob. Long, racking cries that eased the grief from him for the moment, but that could never erase the stain from his soul.

22

The clerk behind the ticket window, a smiling, blond young thing, said, "You're in luck, sir. We've had a cancellation on the Bullet Train. Looks like a Christmas present."

"This is certainly the day for it," Chuck smiled raggedly. He knew why there was, too. Ticket holders were undoubtedly dead. What a lucky, lucky day.

"However," she said, glancing down at Rommel, "your animal will have to ride in the luggage compartment."

"Fine."

What's going on?

Chuck knew this was not going to go over well, and didn't feel like dealing with it at the moment. "I'll tell you in a little bit. Let's get some food."

Finally some sense.

Chuck and Rommel walked across the bustling terminal, Chuck carrying all his belongings in a backpack. He rubbed his beard. Probably time to do something else with it. Trim it into a moustache or something.

He walked outside and sitting serenely in the no parking zone was Alex Romanova, at the wheel of the RAC 3000.

Chuck leaned in through the window. Alex looked at him with a raised eyebrow. "You sure about this?"

"I'm sure."

"I'm surprised you're not trying to turn me in to the police. There's blood on my hands."

He sighed. "I'm tired, Carmen—sorry, Alex. I'm just . . . tired. I could bring you in to the police, sure . . . and then answer all sorts of questions about myself that are just going to get me nailed. Your own bosses are going to be after you, so I feel as if the scales are balanced there—well, maybe not. But as balanced as they're going to be. By the same token, I can't just stand by and know that you're in danger and not do something about it. So take Rac. You'll have a better shot at surviving with her."

"Why, Charles," said Rac primly. " 'Her'? Not 'it'?"

He smiled and said nothing.

"I thought I was dead when I fell off the bridge," Alex said. "You could've just let me fall and have done with it then."

"No," he said softly. "I couldn't."

She stared at him for a long moment. "No. I don't suppose you could have. Killing him killed you, didn't it. You had no choice. You know that."

"I like to think that there's always choices," Chuck said. "A pleasant kid's fantasy—like intercepting a pass and winning the game for your team. Kid's fantasies. Another one dies."

"You sure about giving up the car?"

"Yeah, I'm sure. I want to put some serious distance between me and the West Coast. I'll try the East for a while. Maybe I can pick up some clues about this refuge for psionics I heard of—Haven."

"Do what you have to. Watch your back."

"I will."

"Stay dressed warmly, Charles," Rac said.

"I will."

There was nothing more to say, and the car pulled out. As it did, he heard the first strains of music from Rac. Chuck Berry. Alex was drumming lightly on the wheel.

"*Now* she plays rock and roll," he sighed. "Ah well. That's my usual luck, Rommel. I have no timing with women at all."

He turned around, walked into the station, and, lost in thought, didn't see his ex-wife emerging from the women's rest room and heading over to the ticket counter to pick up her ticket for the Bullet Train to New York.

23

At the bottom of the bay, under the calm, still waters of the Pacific Ocean, a couple of fish nosed curiously around a large, brown, craggy object that hadn't been there the day before. After a few moments' inspection, in which they determined that the object was not going to provide them with anything worthwhile, the fish swam away, leaving the cocoon to its rest, mired in the sludge.

Undisturbed.